A DAY FOR THE FIRE

And other stories

MAURICE O'CALLAGHAN

DESTINY

© Maurice O'Callaghan

ISBN No 0-9549565-0-8

A Destiny Films and Media Publication

Published in Ireland in 2005 by Destiny Films and Media
18-20 Lower Kilmacud Road, Stillorgan, County Dublin, Ireland
Tel. 01 2885281, Fax. 012834015
Website. www.destinyfilmsandmedia.com

The right of Maurice O'Callaghan to be identified as the author of this work has been asserted by him in accordance with the copyright Designs and Patents Act 1988

A CIP catalogue record for this book is available from the British Library

Typesetting and Design Artwerk Ltd., Dublin
Printed in Ireland by ColourBooks Ltd, Dublin

Photograph front cover: Pat Redmond
Portrait back cover- Priory Studios

CONTENTS

To Grainne,
Maudie, Harry, Iseult and Suzy.

A DAY FOR THE FIRE

'Tis a day for the fire sure enough,' he said.

He came forward with his whiskey glass in his hand. He stood with his back to the fire and took a sip.

'No doubt about that,' I said slowly.

He was a neat, balding man, dressed in a dark suit, no tie. He didn't look like a farmer: salesman maybe, hard to tell. I was eating a ham sandwich and drinking coffee. I had dropped in for a quick snack before going back to the farm. I parked in the yard outside. The wind was blowing long and cold from the north-east, had been blowing from that side for a month or more, like a Foehn or a Santana; made you feel uneasy.

He stood there slowly sipping, throwing looks at me. I sat and munched and read sentences of the Cork Examiner between bites. He was probably trying to find an opening to make conversation and I didn't feel much like talking. And the big, empty, cold barn of a bar-room didn't exactly fill you with Christmas cheer.

Especially the carpet. It had some kind of faded, multicoloured pattern on it, with plenty of dust and beer stains and a smell like a loft full of mouldy oats. But the fire was big and hot and cheerful, like a red giant in a deserted galaxy.

'Twouldn't be a big effort to stay here for the day, right enough,' says he, 'that fire would tempt you.'

'Oh, 'tis brass monkey weather alright,' I said, and went on reading. He was probably trying to figure out what I did: didn't look like a farmer although dressed like one. What the hell could I be? He looked inquisitive: 'They say that bleddy wind blows straight across northern Europe from Latvia or Moldovia or some bleddy place, and the first high ground it hits is Nottingham, England.'

'Fancy that,' I said.

'Ever hear the bate of it?' He was half-chuckling to himself at the thought: 'Course if you look at the map you won't find any mountains 'til the middle of England – th'Appenines.'

'What about the Urals?'

'Ah, no, they're further east, tis th'Appenines are the first.'

'You mean the Pennines,' I said, 'the Appenines are in Italy.'

'Christ, are they?' He looked a bit taken aback, regarding me keener still. He hummed to himself, looked into the fire, shifted on his feet and behaved like a hen with an egg. I capitulated eventually: 'Quiet enough around here.'

'Tis faith,' he said eagerly.

'I suppose everyone is out working,' I ventured.

'Well, the way I see it, there's no shortage of work today, for any fella that's inclined to work.' He spoke like the men of the south: a pleasant, thick-vowelled, sing-song lilt, with plenty of purchase on the r's. My accent had lost most of its southern trace but I slipped in easily to the argot whenever I returned from far away. I was at home in these parts.

'Are you from Dunmanway?' he asked.

'No,' I smiled, 'from here, a few miles westalong.'

'You don't sound like it,' he said.

'I've been gone for twenty years,' I said, 'but I'm from here alright.'

'Humph,' he gave a sideways shake of his head, took a long slug and ordered another whiskey from the barman who came and went like a ghost. 'And where are you from yourself?' I enquired.

'Tarelton side.'

The whiskey and the fire were warming him up. I felt more relaxed as well. He had a pleasant, open face; hard to pin him down age-wise. Except he was maybe ten or twelve years older than myself.

'Would you be Crowley?' he asked. He slipped up on you like a sidewinder with the questions.

'Crinnigan,' I said.

'Anything to the Crinnigans of Towerhill?'

'Cousins, I'm from Shanawaddra.'

'I know it well,' he said, 'many's the bad day I spent up there, and the worse night. There's the world wide of water up there, there is so, the world wide of it.'

'There can be,' I said.

He sat on a chair and faced me, getting eager: 'Course I had mighty nights up there too, in Grady's place, and Dan Dribbin's. No shortage of a drop of the crathur in them houses. Yerra what, whiskey and porter, the finest. I knew all the characters: *Jerry 'bove-at-home, Tipperary, John Barry* - I knew them all; spent a lot of days up there on the hill, nights too. I did faith.'

And so did I. Days when the wind blew over Thadies from Carranhill, full of the warm south. Spring evenings when Charlie Jordan's lilting tenor floated up the eastern lane as he drove his cows to milking: *"It's now or never, come hold me tight, kiss me my darling, be mine tonight."*

Lazy sundown evenings as the crisp crack of a hurley ball echoed across the field from Jamesies, and I up a tree like a sailor on a top gallant to see if Sean and Seamus were out to play. And my mother at the beehives and my sisters romancing all along the blackberry roads in the fiery light, being chased by the boys of summer.

'Water is a divil,' he was saying, 'a pure whore if you don't know how to handle it.'

'What?' I asked from the fields of memory.

'Hard to find it and hard to hold it.'

'So that's what you are, then,' I smiled, 'a water diviner.'

'I'm not faith, devil the water diviner, Christ no, boyeen, I'm a grant-man.'

'Ah,' I exclaimed, 'I'd never have guessed.'

'Hard to tell with a fella sometimes, what he does, or what's on his mind for that matter.' I nodded, drank my coffee and said: 'So you know these parts well?'

'Yerra what,' he said, 'Kilmichael, Clonakilty, Rosscarbrey, Skibbereen; I know every boreen in West Cork.'

''Tis a grand old spot,' I smiled.

'Divil a grander,' he said, 'sure there's no better country in the world if a fella had the work to stay at home.'

'There seems to be plenty of work around at the moment,' I said.

'You can be sure of that,' he said, 'plasterers, carpinters; bricklayers are getting a pound a block, man...my own fella was out foreign; he came back. He says 'tis better here than Australia.'

'Your fella?' I enquired.

'Son a' mine,' he explained, 'he spent three years in Australia and things were good there. But he came back.'

'So, Ireland must be doing better than Australia,' I suggested.

'By all accounts,' he said, fondling his glass and gazing suddenly into the fire. He shifted on his seat and moved a little closer to me. 'Course he always was a home-bird. Even though he liked to travel, he liked it better at home.'

'I was the opposite,' I said. 'I'd never ask to come home. In my twenties I spent several years in America; never ask to come home.'

'There you are,' said my friend, remotely, and continued: 'The bleddy fella could turn his hand to anything: bricklaying, plastering, plumbing; and no shortage of women neither; yerra what; batin' em away he'd be.'

'He must be a good looking man,' I said.

'Straight as a ramrod. Finest man in this part of the country...and another thing: a great man under the high ball; don't be talking; hit it left or right, a ground hurler. Play anywhere: midfield, full back, centre half-forward; go through iron he would.' He drank again and said: 'He's dead since, too.' He said it so matter-of-factly it didn't sink in.

'Who's dead?' I asked, puzzled.

'My fella,' he said.

'You mean your son?'

'He did away with himself about twelve months ago. Only twenty-seven. He used the shotgun.'

The patterns on the dirty carpet seemed to grow more grotesque. The dull boom of trucks on the street outside was suddenly louder. The barman hovered out of hearing like a ghost. My coffee tasted flat. He cradled his whiskey glass and rubbed his balding pate with his right hand.

'I'm sorry to hear it,' I managed eventually.

'He seemed in grand form,' said the grant-man, determined to tell me the story, 'you couldn't say there was a blasted bit the matter with him.'

I didn't know whether to press him further or shut my mouth. But it didn't matter. The grant-man had a gleam of calm fanaticism in his weary eye. I sighed in sympathy and asked the reason why. He had no good reason but he could describe: 'Twas the way he went out to the disco with the others, grand as you like. They were late coming back the lot of 'em. They had drink taken of course but nothing beyond the normal.'

"Let ye go away in," 'says he to the others, to the brother and two sisters like,' "let ye go 'way in, I'll stay here a bit and listen to the radio. I'm not tired."

'The others went away in and he sat there with the radio on. They took no notice and went away in. 'Twas a fine night, clear, no wind; maybe two, three o'clock in the morning. They were still up when they heard the car starting, they heard it pull away up the road a bit, couple a' hundert yards. Then they heard the engine cut out; they wondered what was up and they waited. Then they heard the shot. They ran out and legged it up the road. The car was pulled in against the ditch nice and careful. And sure then they saw him. They opened the door and he was lying back like he might be asleep. They found the cartridge...he had shot himself in the side of the head; one cartridge, that was it.'

Eternity beat on as I listened, looking him in the eye. He looked calmly back at me; no emotion, very matter of fact, yet with an unutterable sadness. He liked telling me the story. It kept him in touch with his son; helped him see and hear him, feel his small body as he tossed him in the air as a small child, and the child's joyful chortle of laughter. It gave him comfort against the void. And he had another whiskey and we continued to sit there by the fire.

'There's a lot of it about,' I said.

''Tis catching, you understand,' said the grant-man.

'You believe so?' I asked.

'Without a doubt,' he cried emphatically: 'Kilcurry Bridge, that's the favourite spot, high above the Lee.'

'Like the Golden Gate,' I added.

'The very same I tell you.'

'There was a fellow called Shorten jumped off there,' I said, 'I knew him vaguely.'

'I was there the same day,' said the grant-man, almost gleefully, 'but 'twas the way that poor bastard broke his neck from the fall; didn't drown at all; 'twas the fall that kilt him...and then there was young Buttimore, from up near Kilnamartyra: hanged himself in the haybarn. I knew him too. I did faith. He was only twenty five...'

We talked about suicide for another half-hour. He was an

expert on the subject: motivation, method, aftermath. And it gave him comfort to consider that in the galaxy of the vanquished his own son's burnout was no lesser than other falling stars.

And then I shook his hand and went outside where the northeast wind blew grey across the dark farms, carrying the strong smell of slurry to the town. It had been blowing from that point for a month now. I drove down the single street of the little town: down main street. And Bruce Springsteen sang, *The Ghost of Tom Joad*, on the CD player of my Mercedes Benz: songs of the wasted and tragic lives of young Hispanic workers in the fields of the San Joaquin, way out in California. The smoke from the gleaming, new wood-pulp factory spewed constantly into the virgin sky. Grey smoke by day, white smoke by night, a ghostly fog reflected in the brand new halogen street-lights. The little town was growing up with all the plagues and pestilence that came hand in hand with the comforts of the modern way of life; and death by misadventure.

I turned and headed slowly for the hill country. Up there I hoped we could still hold onto the summers of long ago, when I rode the road like Dick Turpin, on my strong, courageous, sorrel cob. And Charlie Jordan, like Achilles in his chariot at Troy, came barrelling down through the dust, standing up in his cart as he urged his fearful stallion donkey onwards, dark Greek head thrown back, white teeth gleaming, laughing, singing: *"Tomorrow will be too late, it's now or never, my love won't wait."*

THE LORD'S BURNING RAIN

'He'll come on when he's fed,' said his father, as the boy stood watching in the cool of the early morning.

'He'll make a nice horse,' his uncle nodded, circling the scrawny cob, standing in to put his chin on his withers, then standing back to scrutinise the shoulder, crest and neck.

'Maybe back of his knees a bit?' asked his father.

His uncle sucked his quenched pipe, spat and relit the pipe, then puffed. 'Ah, twouldn't worry me.' He bent and ran his palm over cannon-bone, tendon, fetlock joint. 'Twouldn't worry me, a small thing really. And he's straight, a good mover. Unless he's jumping big fences twouldn't bother me.'

'And a good horse over him,' agreed his father, who continued, 'his coat will come on when he gets a bit of decent grub.'

Each spoke as if merely articulating his private thoughts out loud. They worked in tandem, more things left unsaid than uttered. Both experts, one a pinhooker.

'A bit of feeding will turn that horse inside out,' said the hill farmer who was selling. They were well up the side of hills and a necklace of lakes twinkled below in the sun. 'I'll be sorry to see him go,' he continued, 'but I can't see a way to keep him up here. There's not grass enough for a snipe up here.'

'But you're getting the value of him,' insisted the uncle, 'don't be sorry, there's always another.'

'Still,' said the farmer in his heavy, dark trousers, boots and coat, ''tis hard to get a good one, and then when you might have one, 'tis a pity to see him go.' He adjusted his hat down over his eyes and squinted at a hawk fluttering in the updrafts above the valley floor.

'Do we have a deal or what?' asked his uncle with a suggestion of impatience. The farmer still looking away threw his head a little upward with a toss of regret and murmured low to himself: 'No matter.' His uncle spat on his palm and held it out. 'Do we have a deal, I said?'

'Yerra, I s'pose we have.'

'Can't you cheer up,' said his father, 'aren't we giving you enough for him.'

'He's cheap enough too,' said the farmer with humour. The slap of their hands echoed like a gunshot around from hill to hill. The hovering hawk, distracted, lost his focus and his prey, and floated off.

'How will you take him home?' asked the farmer, the pain of losing the colt receding as the crisp pound notes were counted in his hand.

'The lad will ride him,' smiled his father.

'That lad there?' inquired the farmer, 'he's strong but a bit young is he?'

'Twon't bother him,' said his father with emphasis, looking with certainty at his son.

'Where 'r ye from,' asked the farmer, 'Kilmichael side?'

'Beyond that,' said his father, 'over the Bandon river.'

'Tis a long road,' said his uncle.

'Twill take all day I suppose,' said the farmer, 'and a bit of the night maybe?'

'Oh, he'll be tired when he gets there,' smiled his father, putting his hand on the boy's head, 'but not as tired as the horse.'

He brought a battered saddle over from the uncle's black, Ford motor car and a bridle with a martingale. He slipped the bridle on with expert speed and tied the girth to the fifth notch. 'Christ, he's as lean as a greyhound.'

'He'll come on fast on that good land over the river,' joked the farmer, 'devil a fear of him over there I'd say.'

As his father legged him up the farmer asked: 'What's your name boy?'

'Donnchadh Diarmuid,'

'A good strong name,' said the farmer.

'You're alright then?' asked his father, 'and you know the way? Keep the river Lee on your left for about five miles and then you're climbing the shoulder of Sheha. Over the ridge and the road drops down to the Kilmichael ambush and when you get to the ambush you know you're going the right way. 'Tis a long stretch after that but don't falter. When you see the second river you're nearly home. That horse might not look the strongest, but he's tough. He'll get you there.'

The two brothers shook hands with the farmer and mentioned the weather and the price of pigs. Donnchadh Diarmuid sat the horse and listened. His father was a lean, fair-haired man. Lithe, athletic on his feet and angularly handsome. He could ride any kind of horse. He was fearless but gentle too. And he was a crack shot with a rifle. He had to be. In his youth he fought the British in the Irish fight for freedom. His uncle was a heavier sort of man with a large nose. A great talker, older than his father and he could sell snow to the Eskimos. They said he had a woman on the side but the boy wasn't quite sure what that meant. He could tell great jokes with a few whiskeys under his belt. There were other brothers too. All fighters in the old revolution. That was many years ago. His father was the youngest brother except for the sisters. There were seven sisters, and they were formidable too.

With the deal done there was now no hurry, but eventually they climbed into the black Ford, which started with a roar and eased down the hill. He saluted the farmer and squeezed his legs against the horse's flanks and the horse moved after them, carefully picking his way. The farmer stood hulked up in black against the hills and did not move. He hooked the thumbs of both hands into his leather braces and watched a long time until the car was gone, and horse and rider were like specks along the lakeshore.

The lake eventually narrowed into the beginning of the river. The boy kept the river to his left like his father said and followed the sun south. Westward there were mountains and westward there were cattle calling.

For awhile the horse was skittish and spooked at every bird flying from a bush or branch creaking. He had to keep his wits about him. But the horse's gait was even and nicely balanced and eventually he got him going forward at an even trot. The road wound around following the skirl of the river. It was tarred but the surface was not smooth. Here and there lay tracks where the flood had gouged out the gravel. Along the riverbank were stands of willows and of alder; the land was rich at this level and fields stretched away on either side. Hazel and scrub oak grew on the higher ground. There was a smell of sweet autumnal rotting in the air. Sugar beet and mangolds going off. Potatoes too left picked and empty by the birds. There were few people. He met nobody for a long time.

The morning sun slanted from the east casting long shadows from hill to hill. It would be different in the evening. The hills would look different. You'd see new hills in the evening when the sun shone from the west. It would be like magic how the sun could change the shape of things. Starlings in their thousands swooped the skies, disappearing fast as meteorites over ridges to land in some beckoning pasture. There was a smell of leather from the saddle mingling with the smell of horse sweat. There was a sound of leather creaking and a steady clip-clop from the iron-shod hooves. He swayed easily in the saddle and felt good. He was up high and felt powerful. It was always like that when you rode a horse.

Passing a stubble field there was a sudden, fluttering roar as a thousand starlings flew skyward like a burst of fireworks. The horse slewed sideways in a fright and Donnchadh Diarmuid sailed through the air. He landed hard, rattling the side of his bare head with a crack on the road. The horse was all but bolting but he held the reins and was dragged. He held on, his hands burning from the pulling reins. He was dragged a good bit. The flapping stirrups caused the horse to panic. But he wouldn't let go and the horse slowed down, then stopped, snorting for breath, ears pricked, eyes wild. He pulled himself upright, trouser leg torn and with soothing words quieted the horse. He was shaken. He sat down by a small stream and let the reins go slack over the horse's head. The horse bent to drink and quieted further, cropping the late aftermath of grass growing along the sides. That was a bad start he thought. He waited awhile before remounting and rode on into the October weather.

The climb went higher and the road became a switchback, twisting ever upward. The trees were now almost gone except for some Scots pine and Douglas fir and gorse bushes. But there were plenty of sheep and hawks and grey crows. Huge rocks lay scattered around like mighty seeds sown by a giant hand. The wind grew stronger. The views were stupendous and the sun still shone with a soft, yellow, late October slant. He could see long, steep-sided valleys stretching away turning from green to blue, and he could see white-washed farmhouses dotted here and there far below in the townlands of Tarelton, Kilmichael and Coolkelure. Hills rolled further away and became distant mountains. He knew their names from his mother's repeated lessons: the mighty, round-topped Sheha, with its bulging shoulders like muscles on a body builder; Douce and Duchaill, two lesser twins further north, and southward, the cone-topped Owen, which contained on its lower slopes the rocky bed where the lovers, Diarmuid and Grainne, on their flight from the ageing and angry Fionn McCumhail, slept careless under the moon of summer. At its base, the lake like a womb which gave birth to the rising river Bandon, lay calm and serene in the sun. On the horizon he could see the faint, azure blue of the Atlantic out beyond Bantry Bay, and in a line eastwards the desultory towns of

Skibbereen, Clonakilty, Dunmanway and Drimoleague. Even the moaning, singing wind seemed blue. He was lost in blue magic on the shoulder of Sheha.

There were hundreds of sheep, some with late-born lambs, half-grown. The lambs sucked and tugged and pucked at their mothers' teats and wiggled their furious tails. Each to his own. One little lamb bleated in faltering tones trying to find its mother, going from one to the other but none would let it suckle. If it could not find its mother it would die. But each mother kept its own offspring within a rigid circle and denied the stranger. Nature was cruel and organised. He rode towards the weakling to try to catch it and bring it to safety, but it was like attempting to hold water between his fingers. The closer he got the more terror-stricken the lamb became, scrambling away up vertical rocks and bleating like a banshee. It wandered farther and higher and its sounds became fainter. It would be dead by morning.

'You can never trusht the wunter's day,' said the aged farmer, standing in gap-toothed insouciance in his snug farmyard, in the heart of the sheltered valley to where boy and horse had at last descended. The sky had darkened, huge rain-sodden cumulus clouds were building in the western sky and the bright sun of earlier was a fading rose. He sat the horse and felt weary. He had been riding since early morning with no food. His head ached from the fall and his knee was sore and scraped. 'Have you come far?' asked the thin man.

'From Inchigeela,' said Donnchadh Diarmuid.

'Did you come over Sheha?'

'I did.'

'You musht be mad,'

'Why so?'

'That's a dangerous mountain. Look at them clouds will you. If you were caught up there in heavy fog you were lost for sure. I've seen bigger men than you lost up there, fell down gullies, broke legs, and broke necks as well. They did faith.' Donnchadh Diarmuid sat and looked at the old man's striped, collarless shirt and black waistcoat, thick pants with the edges of his long johns showing hooked over the top, and tied into the buttons of the trousers, rubber Wellington boots folded down. .

'Twas a fine sunny day,' he said.

The aged one gave a snort, adjusted his cloth cap and spat: 'It was, was it? Well, look at it now. You'll have a downpour in an hour. You can never trusht the wunter's day, I tell you.'

He looked horse and rider up and down and said with approval: 'He's got a bit of quality but he's as thin as a whip, and weak too.' He waved impatiently and moved with surprising speed across the cobbled yard. 'Come on, I'll make you a sup a' tay. There's some fodder in the shed for the cob.'

Donnchadh Diarmuid looked up towards a sudden flash of white wings against an inky-black cloud. The slanting sun glanced off the flock of birds for an instant and then the flock flipped over and was gone as if into a black hole from which no further light escaped.

'Starlings,' he said.

'They're not faith, nor stares. Them are pilibeens,' said the old man, 'some people call them plovers. They're here early, a sure sign of a bad wunter.'

The boy stood corrected. He lowered his gaze. On the ground

the sun shone warm and yellow against the russet barn into which he led the horse. The tops of the far mountains were now egg-shell pink in the fading light which was being sucked inexorably into the black cloud's companions. He pulled the horse close to a mound of hay and loosened the girth of the saddle. The horse began to chew ravenously.

They entered the kitchen of the farmhouse. It smelt of smoke and baked bread, with a stone-flagged floor. There was a huge, open hearth with arched stones at the top and a wooden clevvy underneath. A black, iron crane held a hissing kettle suspended over a hot, turf fire, contained by a circular piece of iron. There was a plain, deal table with a shiny oilcloth, a safe of meshed wire which held the food and a crooked stairs leading to the next floor up. A picture of the crucified Christ hung on the wall with a quotation from the bible underneath: "*And when the day of reckoning is at hand neither shall ye that do not repent be saved from pestilence nor fire nor the Lord's burning rain.*" The boy read the quotation and looked curiously at the old man. He had never seen this quotation before although his own house had plenty of holy pictures. He looked all around the room again. The immediate sensation was one of cosiness despite the spartan furnishings. The old man grumbled around. He poked the fire with a tongs and the flames licked higher. Then he opened the safe and took out milk, brown soda bread, cheese and a hunk of succulent-looking ham. He also produced tomatoes. On the table lay a pound of Bandon creamery butter with pictures of cows, green pastures and a river on the paper cover.

'That kittle is biling,' said the farmer, 'can you wet tay?'

'I can,' said Donnchadh Diarmuid. He began to spoon the

loose tea from a caddy adorned with elaborate Chinese designs into a battered, tin teapot.

'Did you scald that pot?'

'I didn't.'

'Ah, Christ.'

The old man grabbed the pot impatiently and poured the boiling water from the kettle into it and rinsed it out the door. 'Tay is no bleddy good unless you scald the pot. Not a blashted bit that ever was.'

He handed back the scalded pot. The boy began again, saying: 'I never knew that.'

'Young people think they know everything,' said the old man peevishly. They settled down to eat the simple fare. The old man ate with relish, chewing thoroughly as he moved the food from side to side of his mouth. He poured the strong tea from the teapot into a cup and filled the boy's cup. Then he added milk to his own and threw in two large spoons of sugar. He stirred the tea for a long time and then poured some into a saucer. He held the saucer to his lips and slurped with satisfaction. They ate in silence for awhile, listening to the ticking grandfather clock and the loud barking of the sheepdog outside obviously displeased at the invasion of his territory by the interloping horse. The wind began to rise and the day's complexion changed to a more sombre hue. Sheep headed down long valleys to huddle together under hawthorn bushes. Crows flew homeward to bare and blasted trees. Before twilight the starlings would flit and scratch and warble tremendously in evergreen woods. Soon there would be a vast and songless silence.

'Twas one awful slaughter,' the old man was saying, 'not a

British soldier left alive. Eighteen were kilt in all. One fella nearly got away but he got stuck in a bog hole and they hunted him down. Shot him through the eye, although he was wounded already. Barry marched the volunteers up and down in the blood and gore and then he marched 'em away to the faraway camp in Granure. 'Course they had it coming. The Black and Tans were the biggest terrorists of all. Burnt forty-six thousand homes to the ground in the province of Munster. They shot priests, raped women, pulled fellas' nails and teeth out with pliers. Oh, they had it coming alright.' His cracked voice broke into song: "*On the twenty-eighth day of November the Tans left the town of Macroom, they were seated in two Crossley Tenders that led them right into their doom...*"

His voice petered out. He took a slug of an acrid-smelling, transparent liquid and said: 'Kilmichael was a terrible slaughter right enough. 'Twas faith; rocked the British Empire to its foundations, finished it off in fact. That battle was the beginning of the end of the empire.' He mused in reverie, staring into the fire. Then he lowered his voice. There was awe in it, and a hint of fear at the edges: 'The IRA were no fun.' Donnchadh Diarmuid listened but said nothing as the old man rambled on, swigging the liquor as he spoke. 'Have a sup o' this,' he said to the boy eventually, 'twill warm you for the road.' The boy hesitated and the old man pressed him. 'Poitin is the best man you could take for hard weather. Go on, have a drop. 'Twon't kill you but it might cure you.'

The boy raised the proffered glass to his lips and took a sip and gagged as the hot, hard liquid hit the back of his throat. It seemed to taste as foul as anything he had ever tasted, but he immediately felt a warm glow all over. 'You can't whack the moonshine,' said the farmer, 'have another belt of it.'

Donnchadh Diarmuid ventured more boldly with the next swig. It went down easier. His head felt lighter as the almost pure alcohol coursed through his virgin system. By the time he was ready to leave his head was swimming from the poitín and the torrent of historical facts the old man had unburdened on him. It was as if the latter had spoken to no one for a year in this great and empty fastness. There were stories of the Whiteboys attacking Benjamin Swete, the local Anglo-Irish landlord in 1822 in the battle of Deshure up near Tarelton, when five Irish rebels were hanged without trial in broad daylight by the Muskerry yeomen. Then there was the terrible devastation of the famine in 1847: pigs eating decomposed corpses in the frosty fields of Leamlara: a dead child stretched before every cindered hearth in every house in the barony of Uibh Laoghaire; the angel of death astride a white horse, moving relentlessly onward to claim his next starved victim, in a territory laid waste and blackened and burnt by human conflict of one kind or another for a thousand years.

He stood up and noticed the glint of tears on the old man's high cheekbones. The drink had made him maudlin. 'What's your last name boy?' he asked.

'Hennessy.'

'I'm George Kingston.'

The boy nodded and made to turn away, but the old man held his hand.

'How far are you going?' he asked.

'To Sciathanore, east of Youngstown.'

'*The Wing of Gold*,' said the old man, 'that's what Sciathanore means; a lovely name in Irish.' Then he said: 'I know your father.'

'You do?' asked the surprised boy.

'Indeed I do,' said the old-timer enigmatically. He continued to hold his hand in a vice-like grip as further tears glassed his fierce old eyes. 'They shot my brother you know,' he said.

'Who did?' asked Donnchadh Diarmuid, puzzled.

'Your crowd,' said the old man.

'My crowd?'

'I don't mean your family, but, you know, the Flying Column boys.'

Donnchadh Diarmuid's mind worked furiously. The old man seemed to know a lot about him. He was confused and uneasy. The old man continued: 'He probably deserved it. He was an informer you see. A bunch of IRA volunteers came here one night dressed in British tunics like the Auxiliaries. In fact he thought they were Auxies because one of them, McLeod I think, well he spoke with a Scottish accent. The brother was fooled. He confided in them the names of all the top local IRA men in this area, thinking he'd finger them like, you know, set them up to be captured, or shot maybe. You see my brother was mad against the volunteers. Of course they immediately took him down the fields over there and shot him. One bullet, that was it.'

The ticking clock was loud as a gong. The horse neighed off in the barn. The dog barked a second later. That second seemed like an hour. Eventually Donnchadh Diarmuid found his voice and stuttered: 'I…I'm sorry to hear it.'

'Ah, no matter,' spat the old man, 'no need for you to be sorry boy, 'twas long before your time. Don't get me wrong, I'm as friendly as any black man with the Catholics, but Jasus Christ, wasn't it a fine day they gave him a good hammering, or just ran him out of the country. But to kill him there and then, well, that was a hell of a note, a hell of a note.' He finally released the boy's hand. There was no more to be said until Donnchadh Diarmuid said: 'I'd better be going.'

He went slowly to the door as if he wasn't afraid but once he stepped outside he legged it to the barn. The magic light of sundown glowed all around. He knew the train of night would soon pull in. He wanted to be gone and quickly too. He tightened the saddle girth and pulled the horse out into the yard. The old man stood by. He suddenly looked a sad and broken stick in loose clothes. 'Let me leg you up,' he said. The boy accepted his helping hand. The horse was lively from the feed. He pranced around, eager to go. 'Thanks for the grub,' said the boy.

'A thing a' nothing,' said the other, 'I enjoyed the spin.'

'So long then,' said Donnchadh Diarmuid.

'You're a good lad,' said the old man, 'and don't mind me.'

He stood watching horse and rider trotting away into the fading light.

A whirlwind blew through Donnchadh Diarmuid's mind as he rode along. Black Protestant was a familiar phrase among Catholics referring to the other sect. Until now he didn't realise that Protestants used that term also, as the old man had done. Catholics used the term pejoratively, but to Protestants it must have been a term of strength that stood for something. A badge of identity among a dwindling minority in an ocean of surrounding Catholics. Suddenly he realised why the quotation from the Bible under the holy picture in the old man's kitchen seemed alien. It was a Protestant phrase, something foreign and strange. Although the Protestants had been here four hundred years they were at heart a closed community. Except for their speech. And in this the old man had fooled him. From the way he spoke no one could detect a difference.

The foothills were now giving way to rocky outcrops and bogland with long dried grass the colour of hay, fringing the occasional small lake which made it look like a scene from a western film he had seen in the Savoy cinema in Cork city with his mother. And how the lights of the city haunted his dreams as he returned westward after that first visit. He wanted to stay forever warmed by their glowing embrace. He followed a long, black road through the bogs and as he looked behind, the glowering clouds seemed to be following him like monsters to devour him. Some were red-striped with white undersides, others huge bundles of grey and purple like gigantic mountain ranges, nearly covering the blood-red setting sun. As the clouds passed its face the sun would disappear and the light would drop; then long fingers of jetting flame would burst out again, illuminating the bog cotton to snowy white, casting long cows' shadows across high, green hills above them, and longer shadows of solitary men trudging potato ridges or stubble ground. Like them he felt all alone in a lonesome land. The ghosts of the dead British soldiers could not be far away. The closer he got to the ambush site the more his imagination played tricks on him. Snatches of his mother quoting James Clarence Mangan floated through his brain: "*I see rich Baghdad once again with its turrets of Moorish mould.*" And this would segue into a line from Tennyson: "*Does the road rise upward all the way, yes even unto the very end.*" It had no rhyme nor reason. He found it hard to control his thoughts because of the after-effects of the illicit whiskey. The swaying walk of the horse lulled him into a kind of trance.

When he came to it he knew it instantly. The hairs stood in spikes on the back of his neck. An icy cold shiver ran down his spine. The horse stopped, sensing that something terrible had happened here, some cold current seemed to drift up from the house of death and the stench of blood still seemed to saturate each inch of sodden ground. The road wound around in the shape of an S. High bluffs on either side blocked in the sun and lowered the sky. Almost on cue a flash of forked lightning lit up the landscape clear as midday and a thunderclap nearly split his eardrums. The horse shot sideways across the road and he momentarily lost the reins. Sensing his loss of control the horse broke into a gallop through the winding glen. Donnchadh Diarmuid held on grimly, lying flat on his withers trying to regain the upper hand. The heavens opened and a deluge of straight rain poured down. His feet lost the stirrups for a moment but quickly regained them. He pulled himself up straight but could not slow the terror-stricken horse. Then they seemed to float in slow motion through scenes of ineffable horror.

To the left and to the right he saw rifles aflame with shot and shell. Up ahead a truck burst into flames and British soldiers in black tunics and tan trousers ran screaming and crawling from the wreckage, crying for their mothers. He saw Mills bombs hurtling through the air and exploding amidst groups of desperate men with blood-drenched faces, severed arms and legs. A high wind seemed to fill the sky, the air turned red, a pounding roar filled his head. The thunder clapped, the lightning flashed. The horse stopped and wheeled about neighing in panic, turning this way and that. On a ridge above him he could swear he saw his father with a strange, cold look in his eye, sighting along the barrel of a gun and pulling the trigger and reloading. Except his father now had sandy hair and his face was young, pale and unlined. Or was it himself he saw in some mirror reversing time? Oh, did he see all this, did he really see?

There was a machine-gunner on an opposite bluff manhandling a belching, black Gatling gun, mowing down random-running soldiers like a reaper felling swathes of ripe wheat. He saw the giant Tom Barry, leader of men from the salt-sea slopes of Rosscarbery, bestriding the battlefield impervious to bayonet or bullet, shouting and commanding like a conductor of some orchestra of hell. So close came he to his enemy that the spurting blood from one unsung soldier's severed vein struck him like a rainstorm in the face. And then that man from the flat fields of Lincolnshire or maybe the winding Yorkshire dales, hit foreign ground and would fight no more .

The boy saw the pleading eyes of Harry Kingston kneeling in a field by a fast-running stream and three men standing over him with revolvers pointed, two men standing further off, and three more in trench-coats at a gate going down a lane. As the horse wheeled around again he heard a lull in the firing and saw a white flag hoist, fluttering on a pointed bayonet. He heard sobbing, hoarse shouts of surrender. Then swivelling his eyes to another hill he saw a handsome young rebel, Deasy, the horse-breaker from the fortress town of Bandon, standing up. Beside him stood McCarthy from the high, bare ridges of Knockatonnaigh: The Hill of the Fox, and O'Sullivan the poet, whose family had come south from the plains of Maigue in Limerick many centuries ago, running before the curse of Cromwell. They each stood open-faced and trusting under the stormy sky. But some demons of perversity overcame the stricken Auxies, the healthy and the maimed. They lowered their flag of truce and turned their rifles once again on the three undefended young men, who were even then prepared to spare them from the cold lakes of death. A bullet severed Deasy's main artery under his jawline and he fell with a cry and was silent on the grass. Three slugs tore into O'Sullivan's mighty chest and emerged, shattering his arms that once lifted weights to win gold medals in the sweet summer evenings before the war began. He took longer to die, crawling away, trying to hold blood-dripping hands to his ribs, gasping for breath as his punctured lungs filled up, slowly drowning in his own young blood. McCarthy the mountain-climber would climb no more. He took two bullets in the heart and uttered not even a last goodbye.

The boy saw all of this and even as he drove the wild-eyed horse through the last ring of fire of the destroyed Crossley Tender and galloped away, he could hear the rattle of the machine gun starting up again and the screams of the invaders dying on the wind. And like them, he knew that these his kinsmen would no longer lie down before the marching armies of the Crown as they had done for centuries. And he also knew a wind had been sown that would grow, and be reaped many years ahead in a whirlwind that would change his lovely land forever. Because now he had the gift of seeing the future as well as seeing behind.

He could not recall the roads he travelled from that point onwards but the horse led him. On past Gleann they went and onto the Bantry Line, where they travelled on a flat, straight road to Coppeen. At the three-thousand year old ringfort of Cahervaglier they stopped and he looked back where the last light went west off the black mountains. The great Caha range now lay shrouded, mysterious, with its memories of ferocious battles, and gloomy secrets, dark deeds and tumbling rivers of life. Then he turned and rode on downhill into a lovely valley, with a round tower sheltered by elms and yew trees. Close by an ancient graveyard and through the stained-glass windows of the exquisite little church he thought he heard the chant of, *The Magnificat*, and surely that was the most beautiful of all prayers he knew: "*My soul doth magnify the Lord and my spirit hath rejoiced in God my saviour, for he that is mighty hath done great things to me and holy is his name...*"

And now he was following a silent procession of darkly-dressed people, along the rising road. He wasn't sure where this procession led but he felt certain that up ahead three rough coffins were being shouldered to that graveyard in the night, and he had no choice but to follow. And the priest accepted and blessed the broken bodies of the three young volunteers: Deasy, McCarthy and O'Sullivan, and said that they were gone beyond the painted veil which those who lived called life. And they lay gently in the embracing earth, lit by swinging lanterns in the eerie wind. They were the ones who had killed and would be killed in turn, for a cause that they considered great. But now all was equal as the indifferent stars looked down upon the terrible enterprises of man: clear-eyed Sirius, the brightest in the sky, blue Vega, kindly Alpha Centauri; red Mars of war. And the stars were saying, forget, forget, for time will take away all your pain. You who were righteous and you who fell from grace; for all will be made even in the ashes and there will be no invaders in the dust of by and by.

And then the scene had vanished and he rode on past Brigid's Well and Shorten's Farm. Over the Youngstown river, and through Jordan's Brake until he came to McCarthy's Lane and there at last felt safe. The little horse now began to stagger and could bear the boy's weight no longer. He spoke coaxingly to it and patted its neck as he climbed stiffly down. He led the indomitable but exhausted animal past the warm, familiar high ditches where sweet whortleberries would ripen and burst in July. But now their stalks lay fallow as a glittering frost descended, whitening the winding way. Then he heard familiar voices and saw a flashlamp up ahead. They were his sisters voices, and he suddenly felt reposed and happy and secure: 'Donnchadh Diarmuid, where were you? Daddy and uncle James are home for hours. We were all worried sick about you.' He smiled and said, 'the horse was tired, I had to lead him for the last few miles.' They pressed him further but he would not, could not say more. They soon gained the farmyard where the girls made a great fuss, grooming and patting the tired horse. They brought it water and oats and a huge bundle of hay and installed it in the stable with a bed of golden straw. The great miracle of electricity had just come to the farm and his father came in out of the gloom. He turned on a switch. A single bulb glowed as if by magic and threw light into every corner of the stable. 'It took you a nice bit but I knew you'd make it,' said his father. His eyes smiled a deep, ironic smile. Donnchadh Diarmuid looked at him with tired but wiser eyes. And here was a man he thought he knew but now he did not know. And he would never cross the border into that man's soul but maybe some of the iron that lay within that man was now the iron in him.

A wintry fever overtook him that night as his mother read at his bedside from the collected works of Shakespeare: *"The oldest have borne most, we that are young shall never see so much nor live so long."* As he drifted into a delirious sleep he began to understand the meanings of certain words and phrases for the first time. He would take a few days to recover but when he went out again it was with a renewed vigour. His father was the master who had set him a stern task and he knew he had passed the test. The long day's journey was over, but he knew he was a wayfarer with many more roads to travel and higher mountains to climb. Soon he would be growing to be a man but would he ever be the man who had sent him searching on the road?

TWO BROTHERS

Two brothers were ploughing an upland one cold day in March. The sky was a glum, featureless grey, and the cloud merged with the grey land and the upper air so that it was difficult to distinguish between land and sky at the horizon line. A wind was blowing from the east. It was not a strong or violent wind but it was the killer wind of spring. The upland they ploughed was stubble and the six-bore ploughs sliced through the rich soil turning the sods over like shiny bars of chocolate. A phalanx of hungry seagulls floated above the two, red, John Deere tractors and on the ground grey crows and magpies and jackdaws vied for the fat worms that infested the fertile earth.

The field rose and fell away in waves and this was the pattern of the greater landscape for miles in any direction. It rose in ridges and fell to sweet long valleys. Five rivers flowed east by south-east, such was the tilt and table of the territory. They were called the Argideen, the Bandon, the Bride, the Lee. And many miles northward, the wide Blackwater. High mountains to the far west and north rising in a semi-circle caused this flow and motion of water. When the mountains ran out of bulk and muscle, high ridges still ran on like arms extending from powerful shoulders and between these ridges the rivers ran. This was not a barren land: tall stands of beech and oak, ash and chestnut grew along ditches and hedgerows dividing fields of rich deep soil; and grew in deep effulgence along the riverbanks.

Even high slopes were cleared of rock and stone and hardy crops of corn were planted. The natives here were an industrious breed and left their imprint on every acre. This was mainly cow country and substantial herds of Friesian, Simmental and Charolais were scattered throughout a wide region, many corralled in well-built farmyard sheds. In March, before the first burst of summer bloom, the grass was scant and the cattle grazed on sweet, strong-smelling silage hoarded in huge heaps from previous summers, tasting of molasses and covered with black plastic, held down by scores of defunct car and tractor tires. There were some good-looking hunters wrapped in winter blankets to keep them from the cold, but this was not real horse country; that was a good deal further north where limestone deep in the soil was ingested to provide calcium in thoroughbreds to run for the roses.

The lead brother was called Stephen. He wore dark glasses and he was dressed in an oil-smudged, navy-blue, one-piece overall which would be called a cat suit on a fashion model. He had wavy, brown hair and behind the glasses his eyes were blue and searching. His face was angular and finely chiselled. He was maybe thirty-six or seven years old. He was sitting in an awkward posture with one hand on the steering wheel and the other on the lever of the hydraulic, half-turned, looking back as the earth unfurrowed beneath the plough. There was a sudden shudder as a plough sock struck a large boulder and reared up with a tearing screech. He slammed down on the clutch with his left boot, threw the gear lever into neutral and leaped off the tractor. He moved gracefully, strong and catlike but his mood was choleric. When he took off the sunglasses he immediately squinted and lowered his head because he was blind in one eye where a spike had gone through it and the light caused him pain. Only if you knew him could you tell he was blind because such was his willpower that he had overcome that obstacle completely.

Behind him the other brother, Ollie, came on at a more leisurely pace. He had receding, curly hair, which suggested he might be bald at fifty but now at thirty-four it was but a minor concern. His face was open, unlined and sunny and he played a Walkman with ear pieces to ease the monotony of the drudging work. The song was country-rock and his head swayed in time with the music: "*Left my family in Pennsylvania, searchin' for work I hit the road, I met Frank in east Texas in a freight-yard blown through with snow.*" He was nearly upside the other tractor before he realised there was a problem. He eased up the throttle and climbed down to join his older brother.

'What is it, Steve?' he asked

His brother was preoccupied, pulling at the top link between the huge high-wheeled tractor and the plough: 'The top link is buckled, I hit a rock. Fuck it anyway.' He tugged and swore some more in frustration and Ollie said. 'No matter, we've the field nearly finished anyway, I'll carry on and finish it.'

'What about this blasted thing?' said Stephen more agitated.

'Can't you get a piece for it in Cork tomorrow, sure I'll finish the last of the ploughing,' repeated Ollie.

He was anxious to placate his brother. His brother had a short fuse. And hated putting things off. Everything had to be dealt with today. Now. If it were deferred the wheels might really come off the wagon and the world fall apart. That had happened once before. He watched as Stephen grabbed a lump-hammer and tried to beat the offending, blunted threads of the link into submission. Mould them to his will. But iron and steel has its own will and without fire was not malleable. Eventually he gave up and started walking in circles cursing to himself under his breath. Ollie said no more and walked back to his tractor and continued on up the field. As he turned to watch the backward furrows flowing he saw his brother with a crowbar still trying to conquer the stubborn mechanical beast and bend it to his bidding.

When Stephen got home to his farmyard he felt more centred because it was so tidy; the cleanest farm in Ireland; swept, ordered, cemented. No wife except one who had left him in alarm when she got wind of the control fiend she had married. No children or time for any, just the relentless neuroses that drove him from day to day. The constant hunger for more, the fear of failure, the terror of not having enough: food or money or even breath. The terror of death. Stalking him through cold, wet Novembers, freezing Februaries, warm Julys and crisp clear-sky Septembers.

But there was no shortage of money. His father was a careful, frugal man and his father before him. The Burtons had the name of money, and land. Lots of good land: three hundred acres. And when the brothers were in their mid-twenties the father had bought more, a hundred acres on an outside farm. This he had given to Stephen, with another hundred hived off from Ollie who had the home place. And so they had equal shares with no other troublesome siblings to have to share it with.

But even this rankled with Stephen. He was the first-born, he should have got the home place. But Ollie was now installed there with a lovely, strong young wife. Stephen rose daily in his pristine loneliness and an angry unease gnawed at his insides. Spartan and well-constructed as his new house was, it could not compare with the place where he was born, where his memories were locked, where his centre lay. Its great oaks and elms lined the avenue to his heart. The mystic river Bandon that flowed through its bottom fields was the waterway that kept his own blood pumping in his veins. He cherished every brake and burren, and knew each bend on every lane, each riverbend. And the ultimate distress was the thought of Ollie's unborn offspring, bestriding the beloved turf, and not his own, never known. And if Ollie increased and multiplied so would the name of Stephen wane with each pale moon's turning. And that was woe, and sorrow, and affliction. And what he was lamenting was not only his own displacement but that of his seed and breed, and for those nameless wraiths he drove himself in daily flagellation.

And yet he loved his sleepy brother as himself, for Ollie was an easy man to love. Smiling, willing, warm and generous, and giving of himself. Never one to contradict or seek to take the higher ground, beloved of women but not one to flaunt his handsome features.

Ollie's wife was a dark-haired beauty with sensuously turned hips and buttocks, and tapering, elegant legs. When she wore one of her simple summer dresses her figure seemed to flow in a curvilinear line that could awaken fires of lust in even the most jaded of men or even a man who was blind. She and Ollie were still in the spring and full freshness of their union and so he was a contented man. He was happy in his work and he liked the heft and feel of working with his hands. A man of the earth and seeming to grow out of it, like one of the oak trees that shaded the lovely old twin-roofed, granite farmhouse of home. And he could have built it from the ground himself, such ease had he with trowel, plane and hammer. Though money wasn't scarce it was not a commodity he craved and could survive without it because of his mastery and control of the workings of the world around him. And so others felt happy and secure while he was in their company.

But his brother's increasing petulance filled him with foreboding. His moods were swinging wilder by the day. And Ollie felt for him and felt the daily pain that Stephen endured in his blind eye and felt somehow his darker, psychic pain, though he himself had no such burdens to endure. And the nagging doubt was always there that Stephen's blindness was no accident, as the story went, but self-inflicted in some ungoverned rage. He remembered that day well and the bloody spike when he came upon it and his brother wandering in mute incoherence across the frenzied wood. His wife would always urge him to keep his distance from Stephen, to cut off contact, let Stephen paddle his own canoe. But Ollie could only shrug and say: 'But he's my brother, where can he go? Or me, if it comes to that?'

The ploughed fields soon were harrowed, corndrilled and planted. A heavy roller made the curving acres smooth and undulating, made them roll away like sand dunes to the sky.

March turned to April and the cuckoo came. Rain fell and swelled
the rivers and soon the fields were green with growing wheat.
New buds appeared to compete with the rising corn, and soon the
ditches burst with burdock, pennyroyal, and germander speedwell.
And the brothers worked to spray and clear the wheat of
redshank, thistle, dockleaf and hemp nettle. The beeches and the
hedges were a-chatter with rook and redbreast building nests and
soon the yellow furze of May burst out across the hillsides. June
smelt of new-mown hay and the sweeter smell of silage in the
barns. The cuckoo departed in July and fat, contented cattle
grazed long grasses and chewed the cud into the sun-drenched
evenings. An autumn feel crept into August and then the wheat
was ripe for felling in September's bright blue weather. Prairies of
gold carried the eye to the horizon in all directions.

Stephen again took the lead and guided the yellow, New
Holland combine harvester through the swaying ocean of grain.
Despite his damaged eye he had an artist's silken touch at the
controls. It had been a good year but here and there a patch was
lodged and fallen, yet he would so dextrously move the blade that
no stalk lay uncut and every grain was gobbled up into the
churning drum. He was edgy as he always was when matters of
great moment were at hand, and a good safe harvest was the
bedrock to take them forward into the coming year, to pay the
bank and settle debts with small suppliers. And as usual he was full
of ennui, expecting the worst even when a fair wind was blowing.
And now the wind blew gently from the south and promised many
days of heaven to have things saved and stored.

Ollie followed with a tractor, towing a huge, ten-ton trailer to
collect the grain at the end of every headland when the tank of

the harvester was full. The tape was playing in his ears and he knew the words of every song from playing all summer long. The tape was now so torn and frayed from overuse that soon he feared it would crack altogether and leave only the memory of the melodies ringing in his ears.

Stephen was up ahead and the harvester was stopped, waiting for Ollie to catch up. He looked back in agitation and beckoned to his brother to hurry. The fact that Ollie enjoyed playing music while he worked irritated him no end. And Ollie was slow arriving. Stephen fumed silently. What if the weather broke and the harvest broke with it? One of these days he would take that blasted Walkman and grind it underfoot. Still no sign of Ollie. He slammed the harvester into reverse gear and began backing down the slope towards his easy-going brother. Ollie looked up the last minute and swerved to avoid colliding with the juggernaut coming down. He stopped the tractor in alarm and shouted across to Stephen who was trying to line up the chute of the harvester to expel the grain from the tank into the trailer.

'What's going on?' he said.

'For Christ's sake will you take that thing out of your ears and look where you're going,' shouted Stephen in a rage above the roar of the engines.

'What's your hurry?' asked Ollie with a smile.

'Hurry,' fumed Stephen, 'will you look at them clouds, that sky. We'll get rain I tell you!'

'The forecast is good for two more weeks at least,' said Ollie.

'Fuck the forecast,' roared Stephen, 'when was it ever right?'

And a vein beginning to throb ominously on his temple. His fit was coming on again and he could not, would not control it. He began tugging at the chute as the auger spun the grain out in an arc like stars in a spiral galaxy. He swung the heavy chute this way and that as a jet of grain went over the edge and out into the rumpled straw: 'Will you line the fucker up,' he roared.

'Can you calm down,' said Ollie, 'swing it slowly and she's bang on.'

'Move that tractor I tell you, the trailer's off line.' Stephen was working himself up into a frenzy.

'What's there to move?' asked Ollie, 'if you take it easy you'll have no problem.'

'Move it,' insisted Stephen above the roaring din of the whirling drum, the clattering blade, and the smoking engines.

'Move it yourself.' said Ollie, finally.

Stephen was beside himself with fury now.

'What did you say?' he demanded, spittle twisting out of his mouth.

'Move it yourself if you think you can do better.'

'Right,' shouted Stephen and jumped off the harvester and charged towards the tractor, leaving the still churning chute spouting grain into the air like an oil well that has blown its top. He was up on the step of the cab before Ollie had time to leave the seat. Gushes of grain came raining down to cover them in a grand, demented squandering.

'Get out of my way,' he frothed.

'Will you calm down,' said Ollie, seeing the crazed whites of Stephen's eyes.

'If you don't move I'll fucking kill you, look we're losing the harvest.' He felt a panic and a choking sensation in his chest. He grabbed the lump-hammer out of the toolbox behind the tractor seat and tried to shove Ollie off.

'Don't push me,' said Ollie,

'Move,' roared Stephen now completely unhinged.

'I'll move when I'm ready,' said Ollie, calmly looking him in the eye. Ollie's calmness was like a red rag to a bull.

'By Jesus...' said Stephen and his grip clenched and unclenched on the hammer till the whites of his knuckles showed.

'Look,' said Ollie, 'I'm sick to death of you and your bloody moods. From now on you back off and leave me to do things my way. I should have listened to my wife...I'll be having my own family to look after...'

Ollie bit off his words and said no more. He stared at Stephen who stared ahead as if he were counting years. As if aware of a new generation yapping at his heels and no place left for him to reap and sow. His brain no longer controlled the actions of his limbs and he felt himself free falling. He whispered low and trance-like: 'That brazen jade...'

As Ollie's back was turning to get off, Stephen swung the hammer and crashed it full force against Ollie's undefended skull. Ollie fell forward with a groan against the side-door of the cab as the Walkman came undone from around his neck and pitched through the air. Then he slowly toppled out and down over the step onto the swathes of straw. He lay moaning on the ground for a few seconds with blood pumping from a great hole in the back of his head. He struggled for a few moments, raised his head and then slumped and lay very still. The turning auger was now only raining the last grains from the empty trailer gently onto the naked field.

Stephen stopped, shocked and trembling. He hesitated for a second looking down at Ollie. His eyes bulged and glazed over. He wrung his hands and rubbed his mouth with his brother's spattered blood. He looked at the hammer that could make no impression on cold steel but sadly could make short shrift of human bones. He let the hammer fall. Then he turned off the tractor engine and climbed down the other side. His knees were weak and shaking. Like a man in a dream and mumbling incoherently he sloshed through the wasted mounds of grain and climbed up and turned off the engine of the harvester. Too late.

There was a vast silence. Then he became aware of the cooling metal of the engines, clinking and coughing down. Then a sigh of wind and a bird calling. He looked across the valley to where the calm, full waters of the Bandon glided gently down past Kilmacsimon Quay and onwards to Kinsale. He looked back up the headland to where five standing stones that had stood there for five thousand years looked back at him like mute, rebuking witnesses to his desperate deed. And his faltering heart was already saying goodbye to the lonesome trees and the wide farms he would not see again. The evening sun shone down upon the half-mown hill and Ollie lay in his drying blood among the rows of corn. A few curious crows began to gather, flying high overhead in the silence and then came down to land. And when Stephen bent in to look his last on Ollie the only sound he heard was the tape beneath the wheel whirring down to standstill. He straightened, picking up a fistful of profligate wheat and let it slowly trickle through his bloody fingers. The long shadows of the standing stones cast by the setting sun had almost reached his feet.

TULL

He lay on his rough bed sleeping in his clothes surrounded by the pigs. Sow and piglets quivering together in the warmth. He turned and groaned and the cold morning light seeped in through the holes in the tattered roof which was a collection of slates gone awry and barely held together by flattened back pieces of lead, holding out rain and sky and the terror of a million turbulent stars in the sky at night. The sow began in comforting grunts increasing to a steady rhythm; piglets like elemental, uncaring machines tearing at her teats with bites and pucks and screeches.

He rolled slowly over, smelling his unwashed and musty skin underneath the cotton, collarless shirt, black waistcoat and heavy, tweed pants. He threw the blanket off and it sagged on the horse-hair mattress. His rude pillow held the imprint of his head. His legs he threw over, vacating the narrow bunk and he sat and rubbed his bloodshot eyes and felt his week of stubbled chin. He watched the suckling pigs through sleepy eyes and then he stood up, alone and cold in the clinging terror of the morning. He felt the weight of fifty years and no amount of scratching could keep that monstrous feeling out.

He drank tea from a brown-stained mug and stepped a few paces away from the door. The smell of pigs and dung, sweet and comforting receded and the air he breathed was pure and heavy with impending rain. He began to feel better, insinuating himself into another day in eternity, solitary, under grey clouds tumbling like massive balloons on the peaked mountains that marched along the distant horizon.

Outside, the shack looked tumbledown: stone-faced with one red door. A habitation fit for animals but Tull had no choice but to share it. It had a chimney and when he lit the fire inside smoke would curl upward into the blue and frosty sky to make the world look like a picture from a postcard. A heap of turf propped up one gable. Cobblestones made a paving from the shack to a rusty hayshed. A good-looking horse cropped the grass. He was not a big horse, more of a cob but he had quality. Clean limbs and a straight mover. A short back and a long, curving neck with a small and comely head. A black and white collie with an eager, intelligent face kept a sharp vigil, sitting up on its hind legs like a sentry. A cart sat with shafts upturned. A lane wound its way between high ditches to a white road that ran toward the foothills of the mountains. Children's voices echoed from around a bend, then into full view they came. He heard their cheerful cackles and whispers: 'Tull is up, he's cross today ... Tull is mad ...he got a belt in the head from the Blueshirts.'

He looked and he was sad, how little did they know. But they were only children and what do children know of the world's mean ways?

The children passed on in their cloth caps and bare feet and school sacks and soon were out of sight, confident and secure under the clearing clouds and the south-west wind. He called and the horse abandoned the furze bushes he was eating and nuzzled into the bucket for the remains of the oats rattling at the bottom. Meagre reward. Tull slipped the winkers on and tied the chinstrap. Then he heaved up collar and hames and lashed the straps and tightened; then straddle and britchin over the rump. He backed the horse with coaxing clicks of his tongue in under the shafts and quickly hooked chain links to shafts and chain draughts to collar hooks. He would need yellow meal today for his pigs and rolled oats for his horse; this called for a trip to the village. He left his farrow and the dog followed as he stood up in the cart like a charioteer, not like in his young days but still dashing, and cracked his whip as the horse took off at a gallop.

Tull always went at a gallop. He rushed through life from one disaster to the next. Pell-mell he came down Harvey's Hill, leaning bow-legged into the plunging turns. A horse would not stop with Tull on the driving reins. It would be afraid to stop. But then Tull always kept a nice horse, with a good bit of blood; that could run for hours and be well balanced, with good wind and outlook. He tried to feed the horse better than himself, but some days he had no money to feed it and that broke his heart. He soon caught up with the children who scattered in thrilling terror as horse and cart and driver hurtled over the Belrose River bridge. Boys and girls screamed, leaped aside and shook their hands in mock anger and alarm. A regular ritual. They loved the days Tull was going to town. 'Yahoo, Tull,' rose a screeching chorus.

'Get up, ye kidnappers,' he roared in mock outrage, passing in a blur of speed as the iron wheels spat stones into the ditches and the iron hooves peppered the rutted surface of the road with sparks. A rumbling, clanging, clippetty-clopping crescendo that rose and fell away like the climax of a symphony. Some of the bolder boys gave frantic chase and kept up a tirade of defiance: 'Don't fall out Tull or you'll break your neck.'

Tull presented a fearsome sight. Tall and lean with a hawk-like nose and prominent lips, his longish hair now going grey, swept back and flowing in the wind. In his youth he had been handsome and athletic. A powerful, explosive personality. And he was fond of children. He had a great way with them. He could make them laugh and get them all fired up. He had none of his own and that was a great regret.

And that set him to thinking random thoughts as he made his way to the village this April day. As the horse slowed to a walk nearing his destination he thought of a girl many years ago that he had courted at a gymkhana in Bandon and her name was Kathleen DeCourcey. She had fair hair and blue eyes and her father was a big shot with a lot of land. More than Tull could ever muster. Because he was born poor into a family of fourteen and his mother died in childbirth with the last. Tull could still remember clear as day how they all gathered around her as she lay dying and she telling them to hold on to their little farm no matter what wind would blow. But how could they all survive on fifty acres with their father struggling with the drink and mountains of debt as well? And he remembered like only yesterday how all his little sisters had gone to England to be raised like orphans in the black country of Sheffield and Coventry, some only six and seven. And his mother barely cold in her grave. Oh, how her heart would break. His eyes filled up with tears as he tried to remember them. He could no longer see their faces or imagine them grown up. They were always little chickens in his mind. And they working like skivvies for fat priests or rich English families, with their little, smooth-skinned complexions and blue eyes, and tumults of auburn hair.

And he back home, having left them in England, running in the hills with his brothers, fighting the Black and Tans and then fighting his brothers and his neighbours when the Tans had gone. All his life he seemed to be fighting something, and there were always wars, near and far, and fights and brawls and belts of sticks and blue murder. Christ, he still could feel the belt on the head he got when they attacked the Blueshirts at the railway station gates and that a good ten years after the Civil War was over. Blood streaming down his face and Arthur, his younger brother, dragging him away and the doctor saying he might live but with a gash as big as a mountain on top of his head and his brains showing; and the doctor saying he might have trouble later because of that. And Canon Casey taking the side of the Blueshirts and Ritchie Murphy threatening to pull the guts out of the Canon. And the two-faced Canon saying: 'My fine Column boys, ah, my fine Column boys, take it easy now, take it easy now,' to save his own skin, the hypocrite bastard.

And the Blueshirts scuttling back onto the train with their tails between their legs, the train going west and blowing out steam and smoke to beat the band and the whistle wailing like a bloody banshee.

After that he became very cranky. After what happened with Kathleen DeCourcey, and then the belt in the head, wasn't he out of his mind with grief and despair. Didn't he order Arthur and the eldest sister, Lizzie, beautiful, strong and loyal Lizzie, didn't he order them out of the house at gunpoint one night and he took over and nearly ran the place into the ground completely for a couple of years. Drinking and quarrelling and breaking in thoroughbreds, and carelessly burning the best dining-room chairs for firewood and using the best dining-room table in the house to hack sides of beef in mad abandon.

And guns everywhere: Webleys and Colt revolvers under the rafters and a bunch of Lee Enfield rifles up in a shallow ditch in the high field where Mike had hidden them to take on the Auxies and the Tans during the war: fearless sons-a-whores them two brothers of his, Mike and Arthur. Of course Arthur never called the guards after Tull had threatened to put a bullet between his eyes because that was not his way, Lizzie's neither. They'd no time for the bloody Free State guards because they won the Civil War. And Tull and Arthur and Mike, well, they lost it, if you like. Either way 'twas all a sorry mess.

Ah, but Kathleen DeCourcey and what might have been? And the day she left without him on the train. That was the last straw. That put the final nail in the coffin right enough…

John Desmond wrapped a red bandanna around his mouth to keep from swallowing dust as he filled the yellow meal and the crushed oats into bags for Tull. One by one they dragged the bags out and heaved them onto the cart and then went back for more. The crushing machine was loud and humming and it was hard to make conversation in the shed behind the pub because of the noise and dust. When the bags were full Desmond turned a switch and the noise wound down. He smiled at Tull who said: 'That's thirsty work, John.'

'You can be sure of that,' said John, who was taciturn and said little but who had a good few bob in the bank and a nice business going in the village: 'Will that do you for today?'

'That'll do fine,' said Tull, and John held out his hand for the money because he always liked to get paid on the day. No tick with John Desmond. Tull handed over a pound note and John took out a handkerchief full of coins from his waistcoat pocket and counted out the change.

Going into Crowleys hardware and general store to buy bread and horseshoe nails, Tull spotted Joe Canty going west the street with a big, grey Irish draught pulling a cart with six churns. He didn't look at Canty and Canty didn't look at him but they had spotted each other that was for sure. Canty was a secure farmer with a large family and he was tough too. He had a hard face and a thin hardy body. He was like flint. He and Tull hated each other's guts and they had bounced off each other a good few times in the past. Canty had followed Collins and Tull had followed Dev although they had started out together to fight the British. I'll ignore the son-of-a-bitch, thought Tull, but if he gets going with any of his oul politics he'll get a crack on the jaw. He was in no mood for Canty's self-righteous ways today.

Tull was inside under the low roof of the shop, ducking around all the stuff that hung from the ceiling: sides of beef, bags of sugar, sledge-hammers, cold chisels, wire ropes, horse tackling, whittle-trees and the devil knows what. You couldn't swing a cat in there in the dim light and it had a musty, dusty smell.

'Fine day, Tull,' said Tim McGrath, the self-important head salesman who ran the show for Crowley, as he began counting more change out for Tull after his purchases.

'Not bad,' said Tull and didn't feel like saying anymore.

'Pigs are down I hear,' continued McGrath. He sounded a bit too eager for Tull's liking. 'They're not down,' said Tull, 'where did you hear that?'

'Ballineen fair,' said McGrath, rising his voice with the matter-of-fact intonation of a man who was sure of his information.

'First I heard of it,' said Tull, dismissively.

'They're down I tell you,' said McGrath, getting excited, 'half the pigs at Ballineen fair went home last Wednesday. May the lord strike me dead if I tell a word of a lie.'

'A likely story,' said Tull, and made to go. McGrath was too much of a quisling for his liking. 'Ask Joe Canty if you don't believe me,' said McGrath. Tull turned and Canty was standing behind him. Tull snorted in contempt when he saw Canty: 'For the love a' Jasus…'

'What was that you were saying, Tim?' interrupted Canty, pretending not to hear Tull. Pretending to be unperturbed.

'I was saying the price of pigs is gone to hell,' said McGrath, 'but Tull here won't believe me.'

Canty pursed his lips, furrowed his brow and began nodding his head as if he was calmly considering the matter. As if he was completely unbiased. Eventually he said: 'You could have a point there right enough.'

'Since when did he ever have to depend on pigs to make a living?' asked Tull scornfully, 'sure didn't that bleddy man feather his nest a long time ago with the big landlords and bankers.'

'You could have done the same yourself,' said Canty, quietly smouldering, 'you had your chance but you chose not to take it.'

'Hould your whisht you about me and my chances. What do you know about what chances I had?'

'Sure the world knows them,' said Canty.

'Like hell it does,' said Tull, becoming very hot under the collar.

'What about the Courcey girl?' asked Canty, 'you had your chances with her didn't you?'

'Oh, the DeCourceys were big people alright,' said McGrath desperate to defuse the impending row, 'grand people, great customers here, you know.'

'And didn't you leave her in the lurch,' continued Canty to Tull.

Tull stopped and stood back a step and said. 'You'd better watch your tongue, Joe Canty, before it gets you into trouble.'

McGrath came around the side of the counter and tried to manoeuvre the two towards the back door, but his diminutive stature meant that he was no more than a gadding fly around the antagonists, who squared up and reddened in their cheeks like fighting cocks. William P. Shine was up the shop and his high, balding pate, bulging eyes and jug ears turned like a periscope towards the rumpus, forgetting his purchases to savour the action. He nudged Ned Shorten and leant back like a tall tree bending in the wind and muttered out of the side of his mouth. Shorten was peering in safety around his shoulder but still in the lee of Shine's great bulk. The voices grew from low growls into shouts. As they were ushered backwards by McGrath, Tull was saying: 'And I say again, what would he know about the price of pigs or anything else for that matter?'

'I'd know a damn fool when I see one,' was Canty's sour reply. Tull looked at him, then at the floor, then shaking his head in pent-up fury shouted for all to hear. 'I may be a fool but you are a lying son of a loose mother.'

'Now then, now then,' intervened McGrath, desperate not to lose any more customers, 'no need for that kind of talk, Tull, no need at all.'

But Tull was all riled up and the moment of hesitation before the ultimate deterrent had already passed and he was swinging a fist at Canty's jaw. But Canty was the younger man and more agile. He ducked and snapped a straight left into Tull's nose, which exploded in a spurt of blood, saturating both, and McGrath's white grocer's coat too. Then they were clenching and falling back among the buckets and saucepans, and pikes and shovels that went clattering and rolling around the concrete floor. And if they were younger men the damage might have been greater but as it was it became more of an undignified humiliation than a danger to life. But to the onlookers it was still a fearful sight, especially to young Kennedy, aged ten, one of the earlier school children, who had poked his nose in at the tail-end of things and who would remember it for the rest of his life. It would always loom as large as the single combat between Hector and Achilles in his vivid imagination, and become mythical as the years went by.

And the hullabaloo and the ree-raw was rising. William P. Shine and Ned Shorten were jogged out of their frozen fascination by McGrath's hand-wringing imprecations: 'In the name a' God will ye put ye're shoulder to the wheel here before someone gets kilt,' said he. Shine's stork-like legs came down the nave of the shop, as if motoring of their own accord. One of the legs stood on the small of Canty's back to prevent him getting a greater stranglehold on the wilting Tull, and the other leg planted itself between the two wrestling old warriors to establish a lever with which to prise them apart. With Shine thus spread-eagled he was simultaneously pushed from his coattails by the buttier Shorten, who, with his head low, got a heave on like a second-row forward in a rugby scrum. And young Kennedy was darting hither and thither his eyes out on stalks, calling and gesticulating to more customers to observe the fray. Never had the little village seen such excitement since the long-gone but not forgotten days of the Civil War.

With the combined power of Shine and Shorten, the whole shooting gallery of arms and legs was slowly edged towards the back door, with lots of grunts and swears and curses. Eventually Tull was ejected on his hands and knees into the yard and McGrath managed to slam the door to prevent the malevolent Canty from following after. McGrath quickly got Canty to see reason and he slipped away out the front door with his shirt ripped and his cap turned sideways, quietly disappearing before the inevitable gossip-mongers could get going full steam. And if Tull felt shame at the unlovely method of his expulsion from the premises, he felt greater shame and pain at the invocation of the name of Kathleen DeCourcey and an episode in his life that he felt he had long since put behind him. The past can be forgotten but sometimes never completely hidden and it would have surprised him at how freely the details of his long-lost liaison would continue to be discussed in that locality and perhaps embellished by continued telling. Not to mention the story of his fracas with Joe Canty.

'I still say Canty shouldn't have hit him,' said Ned Shorten, now quite voluble and feeling safe in John Desmond's pub, a good two hours after the business with Tull and Canty was over. Shorten was sitting on a high stool in the snug and there was a regular called John Thomas Allen sitting on another stool beside him. Inside the counter, John Desmond was leaning forward with his elbows on the counter between the two and he was facing straight towards William P. Shine who sat in a kind of settle-bed immediately behind. Shorten and Allen kept their backs to Shine and carried on their conversation in such a manner, gauging Shine's reactions by the tone of his voice and the flickering shades of varying emotion on Desmond's face.

'What else could he do, boy?' enquired Shine, with a kind of resigned fatalism, accompanied by an upward shake of the head that made him look logical and wise all at the same time.

'Couldn't he have walked away?' said Shorten, 'besides provoking the poor man.'

'But I thought 'twas the way Tull went for him,' cut in Desmond, 'is that right, Will?'

'Yerra, sure don't you know he did,' said Shine tiredly, 'why else would Joe Canty react the way he did?'

'All the same,' said John Thomas Allen, 'Canty was the younger man; couldn't he let sleeping dogs lie?'

Shine gave a snort of impatience: 'My dear man, Tull Kennedy in full flight is not an easy man to ignore,' He puffed on his pipe and spat into a spittoon, and gazed sorrowfully into his pint. Desmond straightened up and scratched his baffled head: 'Well, all I can say is 'twas a helluva business altogether.'

They all nodded and said nothing for a good bit. Desmond washed a few glasses, and straightened a battered old picture of a hurling team that hung with other bric-a-brac at the back of the bar. There was a lot of dust about, and flies buzzing. A clock sounded the hour. Then the door opened and Tim McGrath came in and ordered a drop of Paddy with water. His white coat was still blood-spattered giving him the appearance of a sad, Dalmation dog. He knocked back the whiskey and ordered a chaser: 'Fill a glass of Beamish for me, will you, John?'

'I will,' said John Desmond, tilting the glass sideways, watching its frothy filling. Before the glass was a shining, black column with a white collar he eventually said: 'Ye had a spot of bother?'

'Yerra what,' said McGrath, knowing the question was redundant, knowing full well that Desmond was already in possession of the facts. 'But Chrisht'll mighty,' said Allen, having observed the niceties of protocol before it was comfortably time for McGrath to join in the company, 'what got him going that he went so far? 'Twas hardly the price of pigs was it?'

'You can be sure it wasn't,' said McGrath quietly, pretending to study the portrait of the hurling team and holding his counsel. His voice carried a hint of smugness and being privy to the real reason for the bust-up he would milk the drama for as much potential as was in it.

'It beat all anyway,' said Shine and took a pull of his pint, speaking to no one in particular. 'You might have done the same yourself, Will Shine, if Canty insulted you the way he did Tull,' said McGrath, releasing some further bait.

'I only heard the bit about the pigs,' said Shine, 'that's what I took to be the cause of the caper.'

''Twas about pigs alright, but not the way you'd think it was about pigs,' said McGrath cryptically.

'Christ, Tim, but you have me there,' said Shine, now completely puzzled and he launched into a loud, cackling laugh that bespoke a situation too absurd for words. The others all turned to look keenly at McGrath: 'For the love a' Jesus can't you speak plain English?' said Shorten in exasperation.

'Alright, alright,' said McGrath, finally happy that he had everybody's attention, and he lowered his voice to a conspiratorial whisper, 'I suppose ye all heard of the DeCourceys.'

'Why wouldn't we have heard of the Courceys?' asked John Desmond, leaning forward again.

'And I presume ye all knew Kathleen DeCourcey in ye're younger days; heard about her anyway even if ye didn't know her directly.'

'We did,' and they all nodded in unison.

'And as ye probably know, she went away to England in her early twenties and never came back.'

'And a great pity that was too, because she was the finest-looking girl in this part of the country,' said Shine.

'What point are you making, Tim?' interrupted John Desmond impatiently.

'The point I'm making is that Tull got mad with Joe Canty because Canty said, in the full hearing of everyone in the shop, that Tull was the reason for the girl going in the first place. He said Tull had left the girl in the lurch.'

'We all heard them rumours in our younger days of course,' said Shine, 'but never heard it said in public.'

'Never knew the full story for sure,' added Shorten.

'Well, I'm a bit older than the rest of ye,' said John Desmond, 'and I can tell ye right now that Canty didn't have his facts right if that's what he said, and Tull had every right to give him a slap.'

'But there was a grain of truth in it,' insisted McGrath, 'I mean wasn't there something about selling pigs at the fair?'

'Oh, the bit about the pigs is correct,' said Desmond, 'and I can see now what you meant earlier. But 'twas the way it happened you see. It wasn't poor Tull's fault. As a matter of fact he took it very bad at the time. Broke his heart it did.'

And John Desmond drew himself up to his full height before warming to his theme: 'There was a big family of the Kennedys and I needn't tell ye their circumstances because ye heard them over and over. The Kennedys are one of the finest families in this part of the country. Not rich like the DeCourceys but fine, upstanding people.'

'And good fighting men,' added John Thomas Allen.

'No better,' agreed Desmond, 'leaders in these parts in the fight for freedom. But after the war and especially the Civil War, things were *trín a chéile* so to speak.'

'Things were upside down, right enough,' said Shine.

'Anyway,' continued Desmond after a pause, 'the family was large and they scattered young. Tull spent a good bit in England from an early age and in all fairness he tried to make something of himself, tried to become an engineer in fact. But with no money and then the war everything was put on hold. And of course only one brother could inherit the farm and the old man gave it to Arthur. Tull and the others had to fend for themselves and they were better at it than Tull. Poor Tull got the thin end of the wedge.'

'You'll get that,' said John Thomas Allen.

'You will,' said William P. Shine.

'When he met Kathleen DeCourcey she was stone mad about him and vice-verse,' continued Desmond, 'but of course her family didn't approve. The Kennedys weren't strong enough in the bank and the Republican connection didn't sit well with some people either. But Tull and Kathleen were determined to get

married and to do that they'd have to elope; and to elope you
needed money. They decided on a certain day to steal away and
Tull's plan was that he'd sell the pigs from the farm at the fair on
the morning before the train left and that way they'd have the
money. But the best-laid plans gang aft aglae as they say. When he
had the pigs loaded in the yard in the horse crib didn't Mike come
out and stop him.

"Where are you taking them pigs?" 'says he.'

"I'm selling them at the fair," 'says Tull.'

"You can't do that," 'says Mike, and he calls Arthur.'

"I can faith," 'says Tull,' "didn't I rear them and look after them
myself while ye were out fighting the Tans."

"But we're back now," 'says Mike,' "and there's no bleddy way
you can commandeer them pigs because they belong to all the
family and they're not yours to sell."

'Poor Tull pleaded with them and said he'd pay back the money
but that now he was badly stuck. But they wouldn't listen,
although maybe they would have if he had told them what really
was going on. But he couldn't. And it would have taken a brave
man to stand up to Mike and Arthur Kennedy but stand up Tull
did, and fought them like a tiger; but they got the better of him
and locked him in the stall for the day. By the time they let him
out in the evening the train had long gone and Kathleen
DeCourcey on it. She waited for him all day, standing out there
on the street. I saw her with my own two eyes, spoke to her several
times in fact, offered her a cup of tea but she wouldn't take
anything and wouldn't tell me who she was waiting for neither;
afraid that the parents would find out and stop her. Tull gave me
the whole story a few days later. The poor man was nearly out of

his mind with grief and remorse thinking that Kathleen must have felt he let her down and him with no way of telling her the true story. Of course she was never to know what happened, and Tull could never explain, because she had a one-way ticket. She never came back.'

Shine, Shorten, Allen stayed where they were sitting and stared for a long time into their drinks. McGrath was lost in his thoughts and Desmond felt unburdened of a tale that had troubled him for too long. Time ticked on. A horse neighed in the street and someone shouted away in the distance. The sun was coming low in the window in a yellow slant and shafts of dust were dancing in the light.

After awhile McGrath said: 'Tell me this John, and tell me no more. Was she, how will I put it, in the family way, in your opinion?'

Desmond pondered the question, then pursed his lips and said: 'She might have been.'

'Poor Tull,' said Tim McGrath and drained his drink.

'Some people don't get any run of luck in life,' said Ned Shorten.

'No two finer people could you have met in a day's walking than Tull Kennedy and Kathleen DeCourcey,' said John Desmond, 'but they were dealt a cruel hand by the Lord.'

'That's the way,' sighed John Thomas Allen.

'Like a bleddy Greek tragedy,' said William P. Shine, wiping a secret tear away. And like shadows they slowly left the room.

Tull returned to his shack and untackled his load. He fed his horse and dog and then he fed his pigs and watched them fighting over the spoils. And he thought that it wasn't how much they ate, but the bloody ravenous way they ate it that annoyed him. But he was stuck with them and they had been his lifeline and his downfall. His nose was sore and his head ached. He walked across a green field that rose in undulating curves to a prominent point from where he could see the wide surrounding hills, north and south, east and west. And from here he could look down towards the long lost farm that was no longer home but was always home to him. He lay down in the calm April evening and the sinking sun lulled him into a kind of trance. He could hear the bees being busy sucking pollen and the eager wrens and robins building nests. He could smell sweet-scented bluebells and see white-flowered chickworth, fragile violets. And his thoughts were turning far away where maybe a child of his that he would never find, might now be picking sweet, wild woodbine, ladyfinger, lesser celandine.

THE TRAIN TO BALTIMORE

It would be a day always singing in his head, a long day, a long, long way away. A hot, sunshiny, whalesong day way out on the edges of the western world: Carbery's hundred isles. A puff-puff, steamrolling, train-winding day of blue light and crystal wind and white horses on the sea. Oh, day in the sunshine of her smile, her only, certain, life-warming, woman-smile. And his chest out with the first T-shirt ever worn in the west Cork morning into night. And the train going west all rocking and rolling and smelling of wood and sweat and varnish and coal. And the seats so shiny and hard you could run your bottom off them and go sliding round and round.

There was Davy Higgins swaggering down the platform before the train came in, with his big head and fat lips and his narrow little pig eyes. And that long, thin-shanked Frank Crosby following behind who always called him "young fellow," and which annoyed him intensely and sometimes nearly drove him into a rage. His mother was sitting on one of the green wrought-iron seats waiting for the train, reading a book by Frances Parkinson Keyes or Shakespeare or someone; she was always reading and he would often ask her who wrote some old book and she would say: 'Frances Parkinson Keyes.' He liked the way that name rolled off the tongue. Shakespeare was another fellow she was fond of quoting: like as the waves make toward the pebbled shore and stuff, so do our minutes hasten to their end...

He was mooching around on the platform and looking for snails to stamp on and looking at the rails and things. Higgins and Crosby had a yellow hoola-hoop which had just become all the rage and they were showing off like mad. He pretended not to notice but kept edging closer to them all the same because he was dying to have a go at the hoop and damned if he couldn't do it better than them although they were a good bit bigger and older than himself, eleven or twelve at least. And besides, he wanted to show off his new, yellow and blue T-shirt that Sadie Davis had left him as a present when she and her son Leyton had stayed with them for a week at Easter time. She was his mother's cousin: from Wales she was, Swansea or somewhere. And that son of hers, Leyton, he had driven his father mad, he was so wild and unruly, and he was always saying in his funny accent: 'Quick, quick, the gaffer's coming.'

Because he and Leyton were always up in the grove making tracks with their bikes around the trees in the mud, slipping and sliding and frightening the calves and the horses. And when his father would come to tell them to stop their bleddy racket Leyton would say: 'If yer Dad's goin' to start in on me oim gwina go 'ome.'

But he was desperate not to offend Leyton because Sadie had

promised to send him a pair of blue jeans of the kind Leyton was wearing: 'I'll send him a pair of jeans,' she'd said in that funny sing-song lilt that was so like his own Cork accent you had to listen carefully to notice the difference.

Higgins had the hoop on a stick and was spinning it round and round, thinking he was great. Crosby was smirking, like Higgins was a bloody magician or something.

'That's not the way you do it at all,' he said, unable to stop himself.

'What d'you mean young fella?' asked Crosby.

'You put it over your head and spin it on your hips.'

'Cripes, do you?' asked Higgins, suddenly less swashbuckling.

Higgins took the hoop off the stick and dropped it over his head and down to his hips. Then he began to gyrate, trying to keep the hoop spinning but he only looked stupid and the hoop dropped to his feet. Crosby was trying to get the hoop off him to have a go himself and they were wrangling and fighting away. Crosby eventually wrestled it from Higgins and started walking like a waddling duck, spinning the hoop which kept falling around his knees. He kept stumbling and falling over and the boy laughed and laughed. He wasn't afraid of them at all and they eventually threw it to him and said: 'If you're so damn good let's see you do it.'

He put his head through the hoop and drew it very slowly down over the T-shirt, waiting for the others to notice. 'What kind of a shirt is that anyway?' asked Higgins.

''Tis a T-shirt.'

'A stupid-looking shirt you mean,' said Crosby, 'no collar nor nothing.'

'Tisn't supposed to have a collar, you dummy,' he retorted. Probably taking a chance calling him that but he figured Crosby was too jealous to notice the insult.

'Where'd you get it anyway?' asked Higgins.

'Wales,' he said, 'I got it from Wales,' and he expanded his chest as he repeated the name, making Wales sound like the most exciting place in the world, like California or somewhere.

'Well, I wouldn't wear it, Wales or no Wales,' said Crosby but the look in his eye said otherwise. And the hoop was spinning on his hips, faster and faster and they were both agog that he could keep it there with no apparent effort. And they were so damn clumsy.

Just then the howling monster of a steam train came thundering up the railroad along the banks of the Bandon river. There was a glorious mist on the water and the sun was sparkling through the white mist like sanctifying grace or something. And the train came out of the mist, huge and palpitating, and it was painted green and red and black. It had yellow wheels and the ground was shaking like an earthquake. Higgins and Crosby seemed like midgets in the face of this gargantuan which was slowing now and hissing and boiling out steam and smoke, and suddenly a screech of its whistle nearly burst his eardrums. Cattle in the fields were running in fright and a horse bucked and careered wildly around with high steps like in dressage, and he had his tail held high, snorting through his nostrils. And to cap it all there were two fellows standing on a running-board like sentries or outriders as the train finally ran to standstill. They had a kind of superior look in their eyes which made him ache with wishing he could get up there and hang on like them and pretend he was doing the most important and glamorous job in the world. And he was going on that train!

He tossed the hoop back to Higgins and Crosby. Their jaws were dropping with envy as his mother stood up and called him. He knew they would have given anything, even the oul hoola-hoop, to be getting on that train too. He jumped on followed by his mother, and a few other people got off. Then they were moving and Higgins and Crosby were running after them and he was laughing and making faces at them.

'Could you fart a flea?' shouted Higgins.

'Could you fart your arse?' roared Crosby, but he only laughed at them because if they thought they could insult him, those were the puniest insults he had ever heard. Then they were getting smaller and smaller, as small as fleas even, and he had his head out the sliding window, looking back at them. There were telephone poles whistling past his ears and wires swooping and diving from pole to pole, as if someone was pulling them like reins. Green fields and hedges and houses were shooting past at a hundred miles an hour in the opposite direction. He was seeing lakes and woods and at one point a field full of white swans who rose against the green hills and the blue sky and floated along as if they were racing the train. Then they peeled away and vanished into the wild yonder and the train hurtled on into a world of rocks, and inlets and tunnels, past towns called Dunmanway, and Drimoleague, and through "The Cuttings" of Skibbereen.

And he was riding on the train going west, and after awhile he was lulled into a day-dream. He was dreaming away about big open fires, brown-baked bread and the clang of milk churns and the rattle of horse tackling in the morning. His father shouting "stall up, stall up," to patient cows at sunrise, cats scuttling after saucers of snow-white milk, dogs barking to greet the postman on his bike. The sour smell of yard manure and the sweet smell of new-mown hay. Lazy summer afternoons bringing home the hay in huge loads, drawn by the Irish draught horses from the high field or the long field, or the field west of the fort. The calling of corncrakes in the balmy summer nights, light of evening until very late, humming threshing machines in blue September days, yellow corn in stooks and stacks in the meadows.

And Sundays after mass on the outskirts of small villages, following older boys and young men in pursuit of footballs and hurley balls and giggling girls in long, summer dresses. Racing bare-back on half-breds and thoroughbreds, pell-mell across the wild farms pursued by furious excited dogs. Down the winding lanes to the black gate, east along the rutted road, past the *poll gorm* where stones skimmed flat across water, past Jones, and Jasper's Wood and up the hill past Tom and Charlie's. And Charlie singing Elvis in the rain. The horses' iron hooves sending sparks clashing off the road and his brother grimly and defiantly and recklessly in the lead, prepared to give no ground and him and his sister behind trying to get past to no avail. The horses' bursting lungs whooshing out air, their plunging hooves and dancing, prancing legs flying, eager for the fray. Loving the danger on the cunning twists and turns of the lanes; the riders ducking under deadly branches that would take your head off, the barking frantic dogs, the startled birds flying up, and everyone loud and shouting and thrilling to the race.

He awoke with a start to his mother gently shaking his arm. 'We're in Baltimore,' she said. He jumped up and looked out the window. His heart leaped up. There was water all around. The train seemed to be floating on water. There was a white house with a long, red roof, rising from the sea like the house of Poseidon. There was a castle out the other window, and fishing boats tied up, all colours and shapes and sizes. A village hugged a hillside and a sloping gangway led from the village to a distant pier. In between there was a boatyard with huge, hulking trawlers hauled up on dry land with sailors and fisherman scrubbing and painting and welding. There was a salty, fishy smell in the dry morning air and the sun was hot. Seagulls swooped and screamed and fought over scraps of fish thrown on the water. Cats scuttled about watching the fish and the seagulls, trying to decide which to eat first. Before his mother could stop him he was gone and soon he was but a distant slim figure, skipping and waving and talking earnestly in grown-up language to hard-bitten men in cloth caps, with faces like brown leather and faraway looks in their eyes. As she watched him from a distance he saw she had that dreamy look in her eyes and as she approached he asked her why she was looking at him like that. She said she was wishing he could always stay forever young and carefree and as certain of everything as he now was of the ground beneath his feet and the smooth touch of the foot-worn pier; and the wonder of this new world he was embracing with such gusto.

A ferry to the islands soon was sailing and he and his mother were prominent among the passengers shipping out. There were all kinds of folk: old and young, women with snotty-nosed children clutching at their skirts; farmers with boxes of tiny ducks and chickens, and half-sacks of potatoes and loaves of fresh-smelling, baked bread. The ferry was old and red and rusty. It was putting up smoke and trundling along, slung low in the water under its heavy load, so low he could lean his arm over the side and trail his fingers through the clear, cool, silver water; so clear and cool you could see coral and rocks and seaweed away down. And shoals of herring and mackerel making fantastic twisting patterns in the deep, dingle depths. After awhile he got bored just sitting there fiddling, so he went forward boldly to the prow. But the skipper, who sat hunched up in the wheel-house with his cap turned sideways and half a week's stubble on his chin, told him to get back. He had a good look at the skipper, nonchalantly steering with one hand, a careless cigarette dangling from the corner of his mouth. His eyes looked bloodshot. He was reminded of that Humphrey Bogart fellow he had seen in his first and only movie in the picture house in Bandon, The African Queen it was called. He would always remember it. He sidled around the fellow and waited for an opening to start talking: 'What's that island there?' he asked after awhile.

'Hare Island.'

'And that one?' he ventured again.

'Them's the Skeams.'

Pretty monosyllabic this fellow was. He tried again: 'What's that one over there?'

'Cape Clear.'

'Where's Sherkin?'

'Dead ahead.'

'That's where we're going.'

'Is that so?'

He thought he'd better shut his mouth for awhile and he started looking at the rocks sliding by and then he saw a bunch of seals sunning themselves on these flat, jagged stones in a narrow channel they were negotiating. The skipper had stubbed out his fag and was standing looking intently ahead with both hands on the wheel.

'Is it them seals you're staring at?' he asked.

'Tis not faith,' said the skipper.

'Oh.' Stymied again.

Eventually the skipper relaxed and put one hand in his pocket, fished out a packet of Woodbines and took one straight out of the packet with his teeth. He struck a match off his thumbnail using one hand only and with the fag between his teeth blew out smoke without taking it out of his mouth. The skipper looked down at him with a hint of a smile and the air of someone who had done a big *gaisce* as they said in Irish: 'Did you seem them rocks where the seals were lying?'

'Yeah,'

'Well, they're called, The Lousy Rocks, the most treacherous sons a' whores in Roaringwater Bay. They'd rip a hole in a boat from stem to stern like a knife cutting through butter. You wouldn't have too much guff outa ya when you were finished with them boys, because you'd be in Davy Jones's locker. Do you know where that is?' He nodded and said, 'Cripes,' and said no more.

He thought he'd better wander back to his mother who was sitting on the after-transom with a smile like the Mona Lisa on her face. She always had that smile when she was happy and when she was happy she loved to recite poetry: all about the isles of Greece where burning Sappho loved and sung, where grew the arts of war and peace where Delos rose and Phoebus sprung. He didn't always understand the words but right now they sounded fine in all the blue beckoning and lonely mystery of the bay: Roaringwater Bay the skipper had called it. He thought that was a mighty romantic name and he began thinking of pirate ships and waves like white horses, and caverns full of mermaids and whales, singing to each other across the water in the golden afternoon. And he figured there'd be rum-runners carrying booty from Horse Island to Long Island and maybe a stately Spanish galleon coming from the isthmus dipping through the tropics by the palm-green shores. He liked the sound of the words of the poems, they were like music. The meaning didn't matter so much to him, 'twas the sound he loved.

'There's an island in Roaringwater Bay for every day of the year,' an old man beside him said. 'Do people live on all the islands?' he asked.

'Not anymore,' said the old man, 'only on a handful nowadays, The Cape, Sherkin, Long Island, Hare, that's about it.'

'I'd love to live on an island,' he said.

'You would until the cold winds of wunter blew up your backside, and you were stuck for weeks at a time without getting off in heavy seas. Why d'you think it's called that name? It can be a fearsome place in rough weather.' He looked disbelievingly at the old man. He would love to be sailing to a different island every day and neither wind nor high water, nor rain nor hail would bother him in the least.

The ferry docked soon after and they made their way on foot past a ruined monastery. They walked a narrow, sandy lane past small cottages, and came to a beach of golden sand where the sea whispered in and waves broke with a sigh on the shore, and the dissipated water crept back out. He raced to the sea's edge and splashed in without a second thought. The water was luke-warm. There were people swimming far out, children running and screaming and splashing and a furious dog was barking at a stubborn turtle that refused to budge. He threw off his short pants and T-shirt. He had his swimming togs on underneath since early dawn. Then he thought he'd better be careful with the shirt and folded it neatly near some rocks and dashed in again. He couldn't swim but he could do a good doggie-paddle and he was up to his neck in the balmy water in no time at all. His mother started talking to some ladies under a large umbrella and after awhile she called him over for sandwiches which tasted delicious out in the open air with the salt sea and the gentle breeze. He thought this was the best day he ever had in his life.

He lay back and dozed in the sun, half under the umbrella and he was thinking he must have the best mother in all the world. He was thinking how they would always go together to bring water from the well, on wet and windy days to bring firewood from the lanes and brakes, to bring hay from the haggard and the haybarn to feed the cows a-milking. He could see her running in her cut lubs across the yard and hitting the high step, and her tears of pain from the great gash in her shin. And he surprised that she would cry and feel pain but somehow believing that these tears were not real, mortal tears but temporary tears of a goddess who first led him by the hand into the morning sun. Because she sure was a special kind of Mam. Always being nice to him and his brothers and sisters, bringing milk and a pair of bread to Jimmy and Julia, the unfortunate poor crathurs who lived in the cottage on the road to Enniskean. And the tinkers; she loved the tinkers, especially Mary Kate, who had a beautiful face and whom she

secretly believed was the Blessed Virgin. She never let Mary Kate
go on her way without giving her clothes for the children and she
always gave her a glass of milk or a cup of tea. And though the
house was always upside down it didn't bother her at all. Because
she had servants to clean up when she was young, she always said,
and only small minded people worried about appearances.
Whatever about that he always grabbed a sweeping brush when
anyone was coming because he was ashamed to have an untidy
house. But she would just smile indulgently and let him at it. Oh,
yes, he was lucky alright, because she could talk to all kinds of
people, high or low, about any subject and she taught him all
kinds of stuff that she said would be useful to him when he grew
up... oh well.

He wandered away up the beach afterwards and began prising
shell-fish off the rocks with some other boys. They were
competing keenly to see who could collect the most and the
business was so intense they never saw the sun going west and
down the sky, to hover over the horizon like a huge, orange ball
of fire. And they didn't notice the tide coming in until it was
nearly up to the top of the beach and a lot of the rocks that they
could see earlier were now covered up and the beach was a lot
smaller. His mother's voice called and he turned and raced
towards her because the gap between the sea and the rocks was
now so narrow that in another few minutes it would be closed
altogether. When he reached his mother, puffing and panting, she
said: 'Put on your shirt, it's time to go.'

He looked all around. He couldn't see the rock where he had
carefully placed it. He ran up and down. His mother had his pants
but not his shirt. He began to panic. Where the devil was it?

Then, whatever look he gave out to sea he saw his shirt riding away out on the waves like it was going to America. His heart sank. He dashed into the water again but the further in he went the further away the shirt seemed to float. Oh, sweet divine Jesus, his first and only T-shirt ever to be worn and admired in a long day's travelling from the east unto the west, that was the envy of Higgins and Crosby and of every schoolboy from Enniskean to Reenascreena. He dashed out and beseeched some older boys to help him get the shirt, but they took one look at the distant, multicoloured speck bobbing half a mile out on the tide and shrugged their shoulders: 'I'm not going to get myself drownded for an oul shirt,' said one.

'Maybe if 'twas yerself there now that was in trouble it might be different,' said another. And they began guffawing at their own wit and swaggering at the depth of their own cleverness. He felt humbled and enraged and fit to burst with frustration. But there was nothing he could do. He exhaled his held breath and flopped his head and drooped his shoulders. His mother gave him a towel to dry himself and he asked: 'What'll I do now?' as if the world was about to end.

'What harm, boyeen,' said his mother, 'we'll get you another one.'

A likely story he thought; he'd waited nearly ten years for this and only for Sadie Davis he'd never have got it. And besides, he hated being called "boyeen" by his mother in the hearing of older boys.

But worse was to follow. His mother, after reassuring him that she would find him something else to wear, eventually could only come up with one of her own blouses. And he was expected to wear that? He felt as if his hold on reality was beginning to slip. Wear his mother's blouse? Never!

He held out all the way back to the ferry wearing only his trousers and nothing on top. But when they got on the boat it was a different story. The sun was now sinking low, casting a red glow across the water, but its heat had gone. A chill wind was blowing from Reenaroige at the mouth of the Ilen river on the mainland. He wrapped himself in the wet towel but soon his teeth began to rattle with the cold and he had no choice but to put on the hated garment. Christ Almighty! What did he look like? A nancy boy? A freak of nature?

Not only was it obviously a piece of female apparel, it was ten sizes too big for him to boot, and all flouncy and frilly. He felt mortified. And there wasn't a single word out of him as they made their way in the gloaming to the little port. He daren't look in the nonchalant skipper's direction but as they were disembarking he felt certain he saw the ghost of a sardonic smile in that stubbled gentleman's caustic eye. Blast him anyway. But then he thought I'll never see him again and the next time I'm in Baltimore I'll have a boat of my own. And with such excuses he comforted himself as they made their way to the train.

Once on board he insisted on barricading himself and his mother into a single compartment and he spread their stuff around on the seats so as to pretend there was no room for anyone else. That was alright until a bunch of people got on at Skibbereen and he had no choice but to relinquish some territory and share with others. It didn't seem to bother his mother in the slightest and she immediately began chatting away to this good-looking young one of about twenty, who kept looking in his direction with a twinkle in her eye. But he was damned if he was going to be the object of anyone's amusement or fake sympathy. So he kept his back to her for most of the journey and stood looking out the open window with the wind whistling past his ears and the smoke from the engine stinging his eyes. When they got to their destination he eventually pulled his head in and when the girl got a good look at him she burst out laughing.

'What's so funny,' he said, 'don't you know I lost my shirt? Didn't my mother tell you, I heard her telling you.' He was very cross.

'Oh, I know that,' she said, 'and I'm very sorry to hear it, but 'tis your face, you're all black from the smoke. You look like a coal man.' And she went away, chortling her head off. He would gladly have shot her if he had a gun. And now all he needed was for Higgins and Crosby to see him to put the tin hat on affairs. With fearful, furtive looks he made his way behind his mother down the platform. At every step he expected them to come round the corner and start jeering at him like he was a circus clown or something. That he could not tolerate. That would be the last straw. Mercifully there was no sign of his adversaries. They reached their bicycles and he cycled home as fast as his legs could push the peddles and reached the farmyard well ahead of his mother.

A yellow moon was rising behind the tall beech trees in the garden and a solitary blackbird was singing an ode to the departing day. The horse's eye glinted in the moonlight looking over the stable door and the night was very still. The haggard and the haybarn were rising in the yellow moon and the world was reborn in his fitful dreams. Mary Kate, the tinkerwoman, with a black hat, rode a broomstick across the sky and she was wearing his mother's blouse. His T-shirt was swinging from the tip of her boot and he tried to reach it but it kept fading into a sea of stars.

Soon a new sun was rising in the east over Farranthomas church steeple and the first sounds he heard was the dawn chorus of thrushes and pigeons, and swallows twittering in the windy loft. He opened his eyes and he saw he was dressed in his pyjamas. He had a quick look around thinking the T-shirt might have showed up but it was gone right enough. He heaved a resigned sigh and muttered shit for it anyway, like his father might have said. Then he went to the window and blinked into the rays of the singing, smiling sun.

THE MARE

The mare stood under a hungry hill, furry with yellow gorse, dripping in the evening rain. It was a savage place, back of the farmhouse, lost among savage hills. And the grass was mean, like prairie grass.

'Where's the mare?' asked Driscoll.

'With the horse and pony,' said Charlie.

'And she's six months gone,' said Patrick.

'Gone again?' inquired Driscoll.

'Right' said McCarthy.

'What stallion this time?' asked Driscoll.

'Kilcurry Flyer,' said McCarthy.

Charlie caught her easy, 'Like a lamb,' he said, but she broke suddenly with a jerk of her head and was gone in a flash.

'Like a shot,' said McCarthy.

'C'mon,' said Charlie, 'we'll get her again.'

Patrick grabbed her a second time. 'Hould on tight,' roared

Driscoll, though Patrick's feet were over ground and the mare's plunging hooves were like pistons an inch from his chest. But he held on and the mare gave in and knew he was the master.

'She's a bad article,' said Driscoll.

'She can be,' said McCarthy, 'but the heart of a lion.'

They made the farmyard in minutes.

'Shoulda' waited 'til the moon came up,' said McCarthy.

'You'll have no moon tonight,' said Driscoll, as he looked back at the yellow summer hills, misty, dripping, almost crying. The darkness was coming in like a train and from the west the wind blew off the Caha Mountains.

Summer, winter, McCarthy lived for horses: breeding, showing, jumping, racing. He'd turned out a good few in his time and though his land was poor and lacked limestone he had a good lot of it: high mountain land with bog and brake. Not the best to gallop a horse at speed but good for stamina and building muscle on the uphill pull. They said the best land for blood horses was up around north Cork and Limerick and south Tippperary: plenty of limestone up there, rich, flat, wide fields. Down in west Cork where McCarthy had his holding it was too rough too, too high, too cold, too cramped. But McCarthy was undaunted and swore some day he'd turn out a champion, limestone or no limestone. After all, he'd been trucking with horses since he could walk, and his father before him, and all his uncles. He could pick out a nice horse in spite of a poor coat, bad feeding, rough handling. He had an eye for a good sort of horse, with potential. He could shoe them, pin-fire them, clip them and plait them better than most. He could spot a spavin or feel a curb or a splint with one rub of his palm over a tendon, pastern or fetlock. He'd bought and sold all kinds of horses from Inchigeela to Ballabuidhe, and from Bandon to Cahirmee. He got them ready for the shows in Dunmanway and Clonakilty and Skibbereen and for the big annual agricultural show in Cork City. He got them ready for classes, and jumping and three-day eventing. And for racing too, if he could get one. But down his way, you mostly dealt in half-breds and Irish draughts, big of bone but no speed. 'Twas hard to get a racehorse down south. You needed a bit of blood for racing and you had to go up country for that. The odd point-to-pointer might come his way but he usually had to sell on as the racing game was expensive and McCarthy had a big family to support.

Eight in all he had, five girls and three boys. They were all good, hardworking children and as they grew up he tended to leave the milking and the farmyard chores to them while he travelled the country in his battered old Hillman Minx - a mighty car to pull a horsebox - to fairs and marts and gymkhanas; race-meetings sometimes, and the coursing too. He liked a good greyhound and wasn't averse to having a punt at Clounanna or the dog track on the Western Road in Cork City. Christ, one year he had a fiver on a dog called, "Oh, Man," in the big one at Clonmel and when he sluiced up by ten lengths McCarthy leaped three feet out of his armchair after he heard the result on the nine o'clock news. Paid out fifty quid, a right bundle of money in the early sixties.

McCarthy would have liked to emulate Vincent O'Brien: 'Best bleddy trainer in the world today,' but somehow he just couldn't get the wind in his sails to reach that level. O'Brien had won everything since the late forties: Gold Cups, Champion Hurdles, three Grand Nationals and a bunch of Derbies as well. The man was a genius and no mistake, but they still tried to ban him and suspend him. Sheer jealousy that was. But O'Brien came out on top: the small man against the old money. McCarthy couldn't praise him enough and to hell with the begrudgers.

McCarthy was a big, powerhouse of a man, wide of shoulder and of back, and propelled by a hefty pair of shanks. He wore thick frieze pants like an Aran Island fisherman that made him look even brawnier and his face would have been forgettable except for the twinkle in his brown eyes and his confident demeanour. His nose was flat and mobile and his lips were thick and sensual. His complexion was ruddy and his hair, rich and dark in his youth was now beginning to recede, flecked with grey in his late fifties. His sexual appetite was large and it was rumoured that whenever his advances were repelled by his wife for one reason or another, he would seek solace with other more willing companions. His virility was not in doubt and though not handsome, his animal magnetism made up for it. He'd proved his credentials in that department by siring eight children. He feared no man and while not political in his younger days, he was a national man at heart. He could take on all-comers in a fist fight or a public house brawl and many's the precocious upstart he'd dispatched with a few swift punches to the solar plexus or kicks to the groin. All in all McCarthy was an attractive proposition for the average woman seeking some excitement in life.

The family ranged in age from twenty-eight to twelve. Charlie was the eldest and he mostly ran the farm now, though McCarthy still hadn't made it over to him. He would when Charlie was ready to get married. But what was the hurry? Anything up to forty years would be time enough for him.

Sally was his adored and doted youngest, with blonde hair, big blue eyes and a beautiful seat on a horse. In between, the other six were all healthy, good-looking and doing well at teaching and nursing. And they were all good on horseback to boot. Patrick had a great pair of hands and could propel a horse over any kind of obstacle in a three-day event or steeplechase. The wife was a big-boned, handsome woman, an industrious worker, who favoured a good education and a job in the civil service for the children. She really didn't approve of horses and greyhounds and such. These were luxuries they couldn't afford and McCarthy's sporting-life tendencies sat uneasily with her. She often urged him to sell the horses and buy more cows, but McCarthy lived for horses and to get rid of them would have been like selling his children. He just couldn't do it.

He'd been waiting for a real decent horse all his life and he felt his chance had finally come when he was put in the way of one by a pin-hooker called Mick Driscoll with whom he did a good bit of dealing. They'd meet at all the local shows and horse-fairs. At a field-day in Kilmichael one Sunday, Driscoll called him over from the tent where McCarthy was drinking a bottle of stout.

'Barney,' says he, 'come out here a minute.'

McCarthy went out to where a small, select group of horses was being judged in the section for the best brood mare, out of a three-quarter dam by a thoroughbred sire.

'Take a look at the second one down,' said Driscoll as they stood watching them going through their paces for a few minutes.

'She's a good horse over her,' said McCarthy after careful scrutiny.

'But the neck is too short,' said Jereen Hayes, a tall, thin, red-faced fellow with a cloth cap and a tweed body-coat, whose opinion they didn't give much for.

'And a nice mover too; good low action,' said Driscoll, disregarding Jereen's proffered opinion as if he hadn't heard it.

'But what about her bleddy neck?' repeated Jereen.

'What about it?' said McCarthy.

'Too short I tell you,' insisted Jereen, 'and the shoulder is too straight as well.'

McCarthy threw a scornful look at Jereen's hooked nose. 'Sure what harm is a little shortness in the neck a long as she's sound in wind and limb.'

'But her bleddy head is on upside down,' said the lisping Jereen in alarm.

'So is Arkle's,' said Driscoll sourly. 'Didn't stop him winning the Gold Cup, did it?'

'Damn right,' agreed McCarthy.

'Have it your own way,' said Jereen peevishly, 'but the man who buys her will have problems with her, mark my words.'

'Ah, Jasus will you hould your tongue,' cut in Driscoll, 'sure if we all listened to you we'd never get out of bed in the morning.'

'Have it your own way,' repeated Jereen and he mooched off to talk to another self-professed expert like himself, who was all dressed up like the Duke of Westminster in a bowler hat, cravat, cavalry twill pants and brown tangler's boots. McCarthy gave a half-chuckle to himself as he watched them. There were minor irritations you had to put up with in the horse business and jumped-up, bucolic fellows like Jereen and his confidant, Jacksie Chinery, were among them.

A good bit more irritating than these two were the broken-down landed-gentry types whom Jereen and Jacksie aped. One such chappie was Billy de Villier-Brett who seemed to appear at every event, no matter how insignificant. He was standing there in front of them as they came out of the tent, drinking a glass of wine. He spoke in a loud, exaggerated accent and was given to snorting with stentorian volume through a whiskey nose as he held forth on the merits of some filly that caught his eye at any particular moment. Billy was as huge of girth as a pregnant woman, and he tapered outward from shoulder to hip rather than vice-versa. When he walked it was with an exaggerated swagger as his knee-length riding boots smote the ground, heels first, toes pointed, like a large, fat ballet dancer. He had the worst seat on a horse in the entire county and was likely to kill himself one of these days with his reckless riding at fences that were generally well beyond the scope of whatever slovenly old hunter he happened to be riding.

Mick Driscoll raised a sardonic eyebrow and spat and looked at McCarthy, who gave an amused nod of his head. 'Come on, for Jasus sake,' said Driscoll, 'let's see if we can hammer this.'

They strode past the wine drinker without a glance in his direction. The deal was done on the chestnut mare after a good lot of to-ing and fro-ing about the price, the drawbacks and the acknowledged good points of her conformation. The seller would spin on his heel after a derisory offer and walk away. Driscoll would then beckon to McCarthy and say loudly: 'Come on, let's pitch him to hell, there's other horses.'

But they kept coming back. Eventually they spat and slapped hands over two hundred pounds, but Driscoll wanted ten pounds for luck.

'You'll get no luck for that kind of money,' said the seller stubbornly. 'Come on now,' said Driscoll, 'don't spoil a good day's work for the sake of a tenner.'

'You can have a fiver,' the seller reluctantly conceded, 'but not a penny more.'

'Blast yer sowl,' said Driscoll annoyed, 'you're taking the good out of the deal.'

'Five pounds, and I'll hold onto her for a month if you like,' said the seller, 'and that's my final word.'

McCarthy was happy with that. Although he'd hoped only to have to top up Driscoll's commission with another ten pounds, 'twould now be fifteen. But he'd have the grazing of the mare in the seller's place for free while he was letting a good bit of grass grow in a paddock for her at home. And besides, he'd a right good feeling about this one and didn't want to lose her for the sake of a few miserly pounds.

McCarthy took delivery of the mare after a month and put her out in the long field above the house where she had a bit of room to canter. He was proud of his new purchase and looked her over in some detail on a daily basis. Despite some annoying habits which he began to notice in her, such as her tendency to snap when you were brushing her or tying a girth, and her ability to whirl on you in a split-second and lash out with both hind legs, more and more he felt that his instincts were correct and he was onto a good thing in the long run. Soon after, he put her in foal to a high-grade stallion and she produced a colt foal the following April.

And what a smashing foal he was. Big and proud with the look of eagles in his flashing eyes: a beautiful, straight mover with plenty of depth under the girth. Thankfully he hadn't inherited the slight swing of the near fore that was a characteristic of his mother at the trot, and while he had her neck, he was high enough on the withers that it wasn't so noticeable. He had a strong, short back, and as he grew he demonstrated both speed and stamina. Whenever Mick Driscoll came round he'd stand back from him first and say: 'Fills the eye, don't he?' Then he'd step in beside him and put his chin up against the horse's withers and say: 'Bigger than he looks from a distance, always a good sign.'

McCarthy treated the foal like a baby. He fed him on raw eggs and milk in addition to the staple diet of oats and nuts and hay. He'd watch him for hours on long summer evenings while the colt grew from boy to man, the summer sun glinting off his dazzling coat. The cows could go slack on the grass occasionally in higher, barer fields but never the newcomer, nor his mother either. They had the richest grass in the best meadow. McCarthy was renowned as a great feeder of horses, and although his workhorses were never deprived, the new colt lived like a prince-in-waiting, wanting for nothing. He put a halter on him at a very young age and they developed a deep rapport. At three he put the bridle on him and got him used to a bit in his mouth and drove him on the lane with long reins to break him in. He finally put a saddle on his back and put Sally up while he himself or young Patrick led him along.

Very soon they travelled out to the shows with their new exhibit, Sally in the saddle and McCarthy giving instructions. They made an impact straight away. Eyes would turn as they entered an arena and would hold on them long after they had left the immediate field of vision. He was considered a good sort of horse or a nice horse, which in the understated language of horsemanship meant that he was well above average and possibly a champion in the making. In that hazardous and cruelly unpredictable world you never extended undue praise lest at the moment of your greatest triumph your prized possession broke down or broke a leg or got a colic and left you grasping thin air, with all your vainglorious dreams turned to sand in the twinkling of an eye.

Eventually they went to the great horse show in Dublin in the fall of the year. To the Royal Dublin Society where the country squireens from the pastures of Meath and Kildare, like Billy de Villier, mingled cheek-by-jowl with small farmers from Clare and Connacht. United by horseflesh and little else. The year they went was particularly dry and sunny and in early August when they set forth on their journey with the old Hillman towing the horsebox there was a blue autumnal feel to the mellow air. The wind blew lightly with a warm caress from the north-east, a wind of hope and longing. McCarthy was never happier. He sat beside young Patrick who took the steering wheel and Sally sat in the back throwing anxious glances behind at the swaying box and its precious cargo. They made steady progress on through North Cork and South Tipperary, past the mysterious Knockmealdowns and the green Galtee mountains. When they got up around The Horse and Jockey public house they stopped to let the hunter stretch his legs. They ate some sandwiches from the boot of the car and McCarthy was full of cheer. He sang the Last Rose of Summer, and told them stories of his youth in many far-flung places. Then on they travelled past Kilkenny of the black marble stones and into Laois where Patrick pointed out the ruined hulk of the rock of Dunamase, sitting like some Greek acropolis above the central plain. On and on past the slender round tower of Galmoy and into the Curragh of Kildare, where they imagined the great thoroughbreds, Roberto, Sir Ivor, Nijinsky, bursting through the mist like ghosts, their iron-shod hooves echoing through the hills and hollows.

At last they approached the ugly, grey sprawl of the south-west Dublin suburbs, in their gracious but blighted setting between the folding hills of Wicklow and the azure blue Howth Head. The first leg of their odyssey was over as they pulled into the car park of the RDS. Pungent smells of horse manure mixed with the musky sweetness of Chanel Number 5. Po-faced judges, dressed in grey-green tweeds and bowler hats, walking with important, quick little shuffles, vowelled to ladies in jodhpurs and bunned hair, with severe, no-nonsense sets to their chins. And round about this last redoubt of the vanishing Anglo-Irish, other mighty men with broad accents, florid faces and hearty handshakes, muscled blithely past, no longer tipping the cap to their betters but impatient to invade their sanctuary and make off with all the spoils. An unspoken aspiration in men like McCarthy, but deeply and fiercely felt.

Sally was up and riding out, beautiful, with her flowing blonde hair, navy-blue riding jacket, white breeches and boots. McCarthy and Patrick only had eyes for her and the horse, watching every shift on the saddle, every extended trot and collected canter. Rejoicing in every well-executed move and groaning with hearts-in-mouths when the horse jumped each fence, as here and there a bush was tipped but no pole rolled away. Gradually the numbers were whittled down to the best of the best. The man who won this heavyweight hunter competition could look any Saxon baron in the eye without blinking or lowering his gaze. Here the currency was horseflesh. The richest man was he with the winning horse, and that man was McCarthy. The judges called Sally up and with much slapping of rumps and rubbing noses, handed her the red rosette. McCarthy thought he would burst with pride.

They celebrated 'til late and McCarthy had a few too many whiskeys. And in his exuberance his eyes began to wander across the bar-room until they settled on the nubile form of a young lady who had groomed the horse in the box adjacent to theirs back at the stables. And perhaps it was one of those occasional lapses into temptation that compounded his confusion and his heartbreak in the fury that was yet to come, in events not dreamt of on that glorious day when he and Sally and Patrick felt on top of the world. He was succumbing to an unnecessary indulgence and he knew it, one that he should long since have satiated and put behind him at his age. But every man has his singular and secret shame and in the expression of it some are more careless than others. In unguarded moments McCarthy was one such man. He'd never forget the look in Sally's eyes when late that night she inadvertently opened the door of the bedroom in the small hotel where they were stopping, to behold him stark naked and rutting on the bed with that self-same, well-endowed young lady half his age. That was such a look of astonishment and of deep and wounded sorrow as would henceforth stay forever burnt into the deepest recesses of her psyche, a dark spot on the retina of her short and happy life. She quietly shut the door and neither of them ever mentioned it again. All was normal the next morning when they loaded up the prize-winner and set off on the long journey to the south, but some of the joy of victory was leeched away and things would never be so safe and sweet again.

After the high-point of the year that August it was all downhill until spring. They had reached the apex of achievement and quickly too and a fallow period was needed before the next mountain to climb. They got offers aplenty for the horse but McCarthy wasn't anxious to sell. His wife encouraged him to consider everything, take the money and have an easier life. But McCarthy demurred and said with a twinkle in his eye: 'Yerra Christ woman, I'm not ready for the bone-yard yet. Won't we be dead long enough.' Retirement would come soon enough, and with it infirmity, the limp, the sable shroud.

Sally meanwhile went back to finish the year out at secondary school and Patrick went on to university. The others were already well into careers and families of their own. Came the spring and hope and faith rekindled. New plans were hatched. The mare was in foal again to a right good horse. This new foal she was carrying would be a proper racehorse, and who knew, maybe a future point-to-point or bumper winner. Flushed with victory from the Dublin horse-show, McCarthy had his sights set a good deal higher than he ever dared look before.

Mick Driscoll was coming round one evening late in April to vet the mare's progress. He arrived in the aftermath of a long day's rain when thrushes were singing and all was glistening, lush and dripping. 'Tis soft,' says he. 'There's growth there,' said McCarthy.

They headed out with a half-bucket of oats and a bridle to the high brakes back behind the farmyard where the hills piled higher to the Caha Mountains far to the west. Late sunbursts were scattering the glowering clouds, turning the sky to orange, yellow, purple: glorious technicolor.

'Kilcurry Flyer has thrown a few right good ones lately,' said Driscoll as the mare thundered away with bucks and kicks and

snorts. 'He's well met with that one,' said McCarthy, before
Patrick collared her again. As he led her back with the others
following, McCarthy said: 'The light is going on us.'

'No matter,' said Driscoll, 'this won't take long.' The buildings
were fading to black as they stopped in the yard. 'Three months
will be gone in a flash,' said Driscoll as he bent to feel the mare's
udder for mother's milk. The dogs were frantic with their barking,
the show-horse worried with excitement and the pony whinnied
and danced and pranced around and between and behind, in
panic for fear of parting. A light came on in the kitchen throwing
a shaft across the farmyard from the window, like sunrise on the
winter solstice, and into the shaft of light ran Sally like a spirit
from another world. And the mare in all the welter of excitement
and the touch of Driscoll's searching hand, whirled in fright and
lashed out behind with both her iron hooves, catching the
beloved girl with full force on the forehead, knocking her
backwards where her head smashed against a concrete step with a
sickening, fatal thud. All she uttered was a single, muffled scream.
From Driscoll came a curse and from McCarthy a loud and terrible
roar as he kicked the mare into submission: 'You blasted bitch
from hell, stand up, stand there.' Patrick grabbed up the reins as
the mare stood trembling, wild-eyed, ears peeled back, and
snorting. McCarthy raised the fallen girl's head on his lap. A huge
gash disfigured her beautiful face, blood oozed from the shattered
dome of her forehead. She lay like a rag doll in his arms, life
slipping away, her breathing shallow and ebbing. McCarthy
uttered a long and lonesome moan, his hopes and dreams
disappearing like water through sand with every gasp of her
faltering breath. His wife broke down and wailed in deep dismay.

Patrick abandoned the horses as he and Charlie stood white-faced in shock. Driscoll tried to hold things together. 'I'll ring Doctor Hanley,' he said, dashing into the house. McCarthy lifted Sally and took her tenderly into the kitchen where he lay her down on the favourite couch. The dogs followed, whimpering, licking her lifeless hand.

The doctor came and soon put away his stethoscope, saying the ambulance would be here any minute now. 'To take her where?' asked McCarthy in a fog.

'To the Bon Secours hospital,' he answered.

'My dear man,' sighed McCarthy, 'you're wasting time and tide. We'll wake her in her own house where she was born.'

'There's still a pulse,' said the doctor without conviction, 'while there's a pulse there's hope.'

McCarthy hung his head and whispered hoarsely. 'Only one man ever rose from the dead and that was the living Christ. Our Sally's not divine, only an angel…an angel sent from heaven.'

He broke off and went to the window and looked into the crying night, and his tears fell like the rain that had been falling and soon again would fall over the thunderous Cahas, and continuously fall on the rising Bandon waters, falling gently and continuously on McCarthy and all his seed and breed.

McCarthy was a man observing himself from a great distance for the next several days. He went through the motions of the wake, the condolences, the burial, and to an outside observer he was calm and in control. Sally was laid to rest beside his own parents in a little green cemetery beneath an old round-tower. The busy rooks of spring kept up a tremendous cawing building their nests in the great beech trees that would forever shade her from the hot summer sun and keep her from the furious winter weather. And even as she lay in her grave, new life was growing with the frolicking lambs and young foals in the meadows.

McCarthy's guilt and confusion increased with each passing day. The cold look in his wife's eyes was a silent censure for the foolish carelessness of his sporting life. The horses went from being the objects of his greatest joy to his deepest loathing. He couldn't look at the mare without hearing again the sharp crack of the kick that took his daughter's life. He felt himself losing his reason and his power to control his actions ebbed from day to day.

So when he felt the rifle in his grip, locked and loaded, it seemed to materialise there of its own accord, and his hands unwilling and involuntary custodians of the machine that spelt the deaths of all his lovely horses. And when the first three slugs tore through the flesh and blood and sinew of his cherished mare, and her foal in the swimming womb, it seemed no more wanton a sin to his divided mind than if he were whittling noisome nettles with a scythe in the cabbage garden. And when the noble hunter felt the gush and spurt of his mother's warm blood in the cubicle upside, drenching his frantic coat, he stood on his hind legs before the harbinger of his fate, his mighty forelegs like the beseeching arms of a penitent praying, as if somehow to ward off the inevitable projectile that burst his thundering heart. Nor did the rage of death and carnage stop at that; the spitting brimstone messenger came calling on the little Shetland pony and three of the sheepdogs who ran howling from the hay-shed in dismay, until in the sudden ceasing of the confounded racket and the smell of smoke and burning flesh ascending, all that could be heard was the groan of the dying animals and the wheedling whine of a puppy who was spared, to reproach McCarthy with its surprised eyes. And as he stood there dimly aware of the spattered blood dripping from bridle, britchin, straddle, and the last groans of the stricken beasts who knew of no crime of theirs to justify so devastating a sanction, a call came from the kitchen. And as his two manly sons rushed to lay eyes on the scene of carnage, too late to salvage one living breath, McCarthy walked through the yard and out into the vast fields to embrace a change he could not comprehend and would surely last a long and rainy season. And the little dog followed faithfully at his heels to keep a vigil and a prayer of hope in his long sorrow.

THE SHILLING

With a screech of brakes and a hiss of rubber he stopped his bicycle on the dusty street. Letting it fall with a clatter against the kerb he rushed into Applebe's newspaper shop.

'Hello, hello,' sang Mr Applebe, in a high nasal whine as if speaking while pinching the bridge of his nose. 'And what can I do for you, young sir?' He was a dapper little man with a purse of a mouth, dressed in a pinstripe suit.

'Tiger,' panted Jimmy, sweating from the long ride over four miles of rutted road.

'Tiger for the young man,' hummed Applebe to Kenneth, his valet-like assistant, and then he strode to the back of the shop with his head held very far back on his neck as if trying to read something written on the ceiling. Trousers at half-mast again smirked Jimmy to himself as he watched Applebe sweeping importantly between rows of saucepans, boxes of nails and heaps of newspapers.

'How are you, Jimmy,' oozed Kenneth, his voice soft and breathy as distinct from Applebe's staccato.

'Great,' said Jimmy.

'And how is Roy of the Rovers,' asked Kenneth, 'eh?'

'I'm dying to find out,' said Jimmy eyeing the pile of crisp new comics and licking his lower lip as Kenneth placed one on the counter with the aplomb of a French waiter, 'That'll be one shilling,' smiled Kenneth, popping the heavy till open with a ringing sound, like a maestro tuning a piano. 'A shilling, right,' nodded Jimmy feeling the shiny coin, snug in the pocket of his heavy tweed coat, precious as a diamond ring in a Cartier jewellery box. He would savour the moment, no hurry, everything in good time, the intense pleasure of reading the comic postponed as long as possible; the result of the football final to be held off until he burst with curiosity.

Kenneth took the bright coin and placed it in the till with that satisfied air only shopkeepers can muster, everything neat, boxed off, hoarded. Although only half Applebe's age, Kenneth practiced the silly rituals of merchants more carefully than his master. But Jimmy felt addled in musty shops. His head felt leaden in the profusion of objects which crammed the tiny space: bags of flour, boxes of salted bacon, wire ropes, buckets, screws; side by side with loaves of bread, pounds of sugar, acid drops, newspapers. In fact but for the comics Jimmy would never darken the door. He was glad to get out of the shop's sepulchral confines and breathe the clean, fresh air of the village street. He opened the comic and scanned the different stories as he walked to his bicycle. Roy of the Rovers would be the last. He would tease himself with the cycling and the car racing and Rockfist Rogan, the English World

War hero. But these didn't excite his passion like the footballers: Blackie Gray and Roy Race of Melchester Rovers. These were the heroes to whom he aspired, skilful ballplayers pulling the game out of the fire, scoring goals from impossible angles. Because Jimmy loved football and he was an expert at it. Big and athletic, at the age of twelve he played on the local under sixteen team. Just this past Sunday he had confounded Carbery Gaels with a brilliant display of power football that had his father and the trainer, Josie McCarthy, and the other mentors roaring their heads off with excitement and shouting for the blood of the opposition juveniles. With five minutes to go the Gaels were leading by two points. 'Come on the village,' roared Josie, chomping on his unlit pipe, as he ran up and down the sideline simulating each catch and kick, with cocked leg or crooked elbow.

'Come on the red and whites,' came the opposition's reply, 'come on the blood and bandage, that's the hammer.'

Beside himself with agitation, Josie fumbled for his pocket watch, 'Only one minute left,' he groaned to Jimmy's father who kept a more controlled demeanour.

'Go for that ball Jimmy O'Leary, you can do it,' exhorted Josie, 'you have to do it.'

The kick-out flew high in the air from the goalkeeper's boot. Jimmy and his taller midfield opponent raced for it, poised to leap. His opponent took off first, both hands clawing the air. The ball hurtled toward them as Jimmy soared higher and caught it with one hand and sped downfield in a weaving, side-stepping solo run. The crowd gasped in amazement as he beat one, then two, then three opponents. The full back thundered toward him, but Jimmy picked his spot and launched a fierce, curving drop-shot that swept high into the net beyond the outstretched fingers of the goalkeeper. The home crowd erupted. Caps flew in the air. Josie McCarthy danced a jig on the sideline. Bud Lordan, the village blacksmith turned to James Foley the tailor and said: 'By God, did you see that. That young fella will be the best bleddy player in the country yet.'

'He is already, he is already,' said Foley.

Soon after, the final whistle sounded and Jimmy was shouldered off in triumph. Josie and his father stood waiting as he was lowered by his friends, Willie Hogan and Chris Connolly. 'Jimmy O'Leary,' said Josie, grasping him by the hand and shoulder and shaking him, with a look of ecstasy on his face, 'that one-handed catch would do credit to Mick O'Connell himself.'

His father watched quietly, proudly.

Jimmy now smiled at the memory as he ran alongside his bicycle and leaped into the saddle like Buck Jones the cowboy leaping on his horse; the way he did in the bunch of Dell comics which he had swapped with Willie Hogan - the ones his father had banned from the house. Jimmy hid them in a cardboard box in the oak tree in the garden with the hole in the trunk.

The street was quiet today. No cattle bawling, no farmers spitting and slapping hands, no squealing piglets confined in cribs. The monthly fair-day was the time for the excitement: tanglers with brown boots and cloth caps arguing with his father, making deals, breaking deals, bogus tempers and furious, vein-bursting tantrums. Elation and disappointment. Taking the cattle along the wet roads at sunrise in anticipation of a large feed of lamb chops at Molly Seamore's restaurant. Wearily driving the hungry cattle home in the late afternoon, his father a little sadder, a little drunk, a little older. But if the deal was good and the cattle sold and gone on the train his father walked with a spring in his step and told him stories of his glory days in Tom Barry's Flying Column, fighting for Irish freedom. And Jimmy always listened with respect to his father because his father was that kind of man - when he spoke you listened. Because he had that authority. Like the Kansas Kid his father could handle a gun; shoot a rabbit or the head off a crow from three hundred yards with a .22 rifle. Jimmy had seen him do it. People liked his father. He was popular; could sing a sweet song, race a good greyhound. And they respected him too. For his father was a soldier, had fought in the old revolution. He was a man to be reckoned with and no mistake.

Yesterday Josie McCarthy had given Jimmy a pound note in a brown envelope. 'Give that to the priest for me like a good lad,' he had said cheerfully, 'tis for the dues.'

He took the envelope as he had often done before on his way to school in the village. He and Josie were good friends despite the age gap. They'd talk about sporting matters, the existence of God, the price of pigs, the advantages of women. Josie was wise in his way, and a great story-teller. He lived in London during the Second World War and he described the German air-raids in vivid detail, fuelling Jimmy's imagination. Although Josie was a wiry man and a great dancer, he never married. 'Life, Jimmy boy,' he'd say, 'doesn't always work out the way you want it to.'

The one thing they never discussed was politics. Jimmy knew all about the Irish War of Independence from his father, but a far trickier subject was the Civil War which followed, when comrades-in-arms became deadly enemies and fought each other to a standstill. Josie and his father were on opposite sides in the

Civil War. His father was obsessed with the past, Josie just wanted to forget.

It was football above all that bonded them. Josie lived to train the team. If he had no wife he certainly had a family: the players. And of all the players, Jimmy was the hottest prospect seen in that part of the country for many a long year. Josie would make him a star. Josie was going to the creamery in the horse and cart and he gave Jimmy a lift to the end of the winding lane. Dan, the horse trotted along past the high ditches bursting with ripe whortle berries. Off to the left was the deep, dank quarry full of slate-grey water. Jimmy would never forget the day a cow drowned in the quarry. A tractor had pulled her out: a red speckled cow who had slipped when she bent to drink. At the lane end Jimmy jumped off the cart and stood watching Josie heading for the creamery on the hill. He patted his pocket to feel the envelope and then he turned and sprinted west on the long, white, winding road to school in the village of Towerhill.

He was agitated all day, scarcely noticing the teacher, Master O'Donnell or the other pupils. Willie Hogan made a joke about puck goats which the schoolmaster did not appreciate. 'Get your arithmetic,' said he curtly, to punish them for laughing, knowing they hated sums. What they enjoyed most of all was the geography class, standing in a circle around a tattered map of the world, pinching the girls and pointing to exotic-sounding, faraway places like Singapore and Valparaiso and Tashkent. At twelve-thirty Father Cassidy came in and asked them questions from the catechism: 'Who made the world?'

'A black pig with his tail curled,' whispered Willie behind Jimmy's back as he desperately, with grins and grimaces, tried to keep a solemn face for the priest. 'God made the world,' he managed eventually.

At lunch-hour the boys contested a furious football game in the cramped yard behind the school but Jimmy's mind was elsewhere. 'Blast you,' shouted the puny Willie Hogan with a drop at the end of his nose, 'blast you, Jimmy, you let Chris Connolly score another goal.' Jimmy shrugged and felt the brown envelope in his grey coat. Four o'clock was looming and a dark scheme was rising to the surface of his mind like some frightening sea-creature from the deep. All day the monster lay dormant but now its fearful but fascinating head hovered into view. Would he break the pound and take a shilling to buy Tiger? Time and again he banished the thought but still it kept returning. He finally faced it and analysed the possibilities with clinical calculation, like Macbeth pondering Duncan's downfall. He had Josie's pound, nestling like a freshly-caught fish in the envelope. Of course his bounden duty under pain of mortal sin was to pay the priest; he was a trustee of Josie's money, Josie was his friend. But would the priest miss one single shilling out of twenty? And the pleasure one shilling would bring him: all those fantastic stories in the comic and the icing on the cake: the savouring of the result of the Melchester Rovers cup final game with Southend United. He wouldn't get another chance to read the final episode. He had asked his mother for money but she dismissed the idea out of hand. There might be money for the Greek classics or for Peig Sayers, or Shakespeare whom she loved, but certainly not for a comic, and an English one at that. He daren't even consider asking his father and Willie Hogan was as poor as a church-mouse with patches on the ass of his britches. No, this was his only opportunity and it was too good to miss. And so to put it into execution.

At four o'clock, school was out. With Willie Hogan, Jimmy left the school grounds and faced up the middle of the street like Wyatt Earp facing a gunslinger in a showdown. The priest in the church at the far end of the village being his opponent. But there were a few stops to make, running the gauntlet of the street as it were, before reaching the general store: Michael Hickey's grocery shop. On the left they negotiated the carpenter's workshop, with wood shavings piled like chaff around the door and inside, the white, shining shafts of a new cart which the carpenter was planing with a sculptor's skill and patience. The sweet, resiny tang of freshly-hewn timber filled his nostrils as he stole a glance at the bent old wood artist with the moustache and great nose. He was a fine old gentleman with a crusty sense of humour who whistled while he worked. Jimmy momentarily forgot his impending decision as he and Willie Hogan continued up their imaginary Wild West street: Matt Dillon out of Gunsmoke and Festis his deputy, from the radio play on Sunday which his father always turned off halfway through. Foreign trash he called it, much to Jimmy's dismay. After a few drinks on Sunday with his hat well back on his head, his father wasn't one to argue with.

They passed Bud Lordan's tiny forge with huge clouds of smoke billowing out the door. The smell of a red-hot horseshoe burning a hoof was sweet and pungent as Bud bent his skinny back and held up the mighty hind leg of a Clydesdale. 'You'll die from the smoke,' grinned Willie, as Bud wiped his sweaty brow.

'There's no smoke here,' said Bud mysteriously, privy to the secrets of his trade. 'Stand here by the fire, there's no smoke here boy.'

It was true. The space around the great bellows, the fire and the ringing anvil were smoke-free, like some oasis in the midst of a desert. 'Lord God,' exclaimed Willie in amazement, 'how is that?'

'Oh, that's scientific,' said Bud, screwing up his eyes and giving a little knowing jerk of his head, 'but I bet you never can't figure out why, smart an' all as you think you are.'

'Lord God,' swore Willie again, 'isn't that a fierce thing altogether.'

Bud winked at Jimmy. 'Come on,' said Jimmy, remembering his date with the priest.

They walked on up the street and went into the grocer's shop. 'My father says that Bud was a grand little blacksmith 'til he got the legacy,' said Jimmy to the knock-kneed Willie, mooching along by his side, 'but once he got the money he drank it all and forgot about work.'

'Cripes,' said Willie.

'Change that pound for me will you, Michael?' said Jimmy to the grocer, effecting a studied nonchalance. 'Change is it,' asked Michael sharply, 'and what d'you want to buy?'

'Nothing,' said Jimmy.

'And what d'you want change for so?' asked Michael, and Jimmy with the guilty conscience thought he detected a suspicious edge in the voice.

'My mother wants to buy a few hens from Mrs Hogan,' he lied expansively, 'that'll cost about twelve bob so she'll need the change.'

'Hmm,' grumbled Michael, as he looked over the rim of his glasses perched at the end of his nose. He went to the till and slowly punched the keys to open it. Slowlier still he counted out twenty silver shillings, tilting his head back and scrutinising Jimmy through his glasses. He wrinkled his nose and pursed his slack lips. 'There you are,' he said ungraciously, 'but mind now I wouldn't do it for anyone else.' Jimmy smiled at Michael and quit the shop. Being famous had its advantages. Phase one had worked. The fact that shopkeepers hated giving change didn't cost him a thought as he walked on giddy legs past Ben Kingston's bawling barn up the slight hill to the church, with Willie following like a faithful puppy dog. 'Where are we going now?' he inquired.

'Them bloody cattle are starved,' said Jimmy ignoring the question, 'Ben Kingston isn't half feeding 'em.'

* * *

'Who's doing the half,' asked Father Cassidy in the sacristy the following Sunday as he wrapped his pale, amorphous body in a long, white cassock, and tied it with a tasselled rope. 'Jimmy is,' said Willie Hogan, 'I'm doing the bell.'

'No, 'tis the other way 'round,' insisted Jimmy, 'you did the bell last week, so you're doing the half.'

'Alright then, Jimmy's doing the bell,' intoned Father Cassidy in his soft, dreamy, placating voice, as he stuck his head through a green sleeveless chasuble and completed the ensemble by swishing a stole around his neck with practised ease. He smiled, and resumed his muttered prayers as the two boys donned their black and white soutanes. To be an altar boy was an honour. To be the one to do an altar boy's hardest task, the bell, was to have the limelight for that particular Sunday. Jimmy stole a sidelong glance at the priest and detected no trace of dissatisfaction at his having received only nineteen shillings for Josie McCarthy's dues, and not the customary pound. Jimmy had given him the resealed envelope the preceding Thursday after getting the change from the shopkeeper and Father Cassidy had taken it without question. Jimmy now surveyed him from under his eyebrows. Perhaps he had not yet opened the envelope? Would he not think it odd, to find nineteen shillings and not the full, green pound? At all events it was too late now. The damage was done.

Jimmy had raced home from school that same Thursday leaving the bemused Willie Hogan floundering in his wake. Grabbing his mother's high Nelly he'd cycled in a welter of excitement to Ballymartin to buy Tiger at Applebe's newspaper shop. He now knew that Melchester Rovers were champions, having triumphed over Southend United after a thrilling battle. Blackie Grey had sprinted down the right wing with the ball dancing at his feet as if tied by an invisible string. He dribbled like a gazelle past three defenders and crossed an in-swinger to Roy Race who dived in at the near post and struck a glancing header past the helpless keeper for the winning goal. It was a sweet victory and Jimmy read through the pages again and again in complete satisfaction.

He was still thinking about it when he got a dig from Willie in the ribs. It was the middle of Mass and the priest was genuflecting for the consecration, the changing of the wine into the blood of Christ. 'The bell,' hissed Willie. Jimmy snatched the stick and smote at the big brass bell and missed. The priest was already holding the round, white host over his head, the congregation was bent in adoration with breath held. Not a mouse stirred as Jimmy struck again, twice, to make up for the first miss. Willie raised two alarmed eyebrows, 'you're only supposed to hit it once,' he whispered, darting a look at the priest who turned half-sideways and impatiently cleared his throat. The boys then leaped into an intricate series of manoeuvres: switching the book across the altar, bringing water for the lavabo, the symbolic washing of hands, and moving the bell up two steps and one over. All accomplished swiftly and with much bowing, genuflecting and kissing the hem of garments. When it was over Jimmy sat facing the congregation, out of breath, his face red as a beetroot as the priest launched into a sermon: the seventh commandment - Thou Shalt Not Steal!

Jimmy observed the people from his elevated perch. Devout mothers in scarves at the front on the long, hard, varnished seats that smelled of musk and incense. He shifted his backside on the cold, marble step of the holy of holies, and heard a cacophony of coughs and a clicking chorus of rosary beads. He saw gnarl-handed sons of toil leaning against the stone pillars at the porch, some whispering and telling jokes, others down on one knee using their cloth caps as cushions, gazing vacantly at the priest with bored expressions. And the priest warming to his subject: 'Tenth,' he thundered, 'Thou shalt not covet thy neighbour's GOODS!'

Goods, thought Jimmy, was money included? Maybe not? Maybe he had escaped the definition, slipped through a technical loophole. Christ, he was beginning to sweat. And there was Josie McCarthy at the bottom of the aisle, ramrod straight in his dapper, baggy pants and bum-freezer jacket, striped shirt and stud, no collar. Was it at him Josie was staring so sternly? Had he found out? Why was the priest preaching about neighbour's goods all of a sudden? Jimmy looked around the church and began to get the uneasy feeling that all eyes were on him. He fought his panic, looking casually away then back again, only to find more accusing eyes boring into his black and damned soul. What a little fool he had been, to think he would get away with it, to deprive the priest himself of his rightful dues. There was Mrs O'Donnell, the schoolmaster's wife, so holy that she had one foot in heaven already, and only a few minutes ago he had held the silver platter under her chin while the priest served her the sacred bread. And there further back was his own uncle, John O'Leary, the largest merchant in the village and beside him, James Foley the tailor, who might criticise the priest discreetly in the pub but never miss one mass three-hundred and sixty-five days in the year for all that. He felt certain that any minute now his name would be mentioned and his heinous crime exposed. Taking money from the priest, the most powerful man in the parish, Christ's vicar on earth. Sure hadn't Mrs O'Donnell often told them of the central and insuperable position of the church in the rural world, where the laws of God were laid down more strictly than by any temporal judge. Sure wasn't Judge Williams himself sitting in the front row under Jimmy's nose with his eleven children, all poker-faced and scrubbed, still trying to swallow their holy communion that clung like chewing gum to the roofs of their mouths. He looked around despairingly as the priest wound down his sermon at these devout and upright citizens, pillars of the church – what pillars? - the very church itself - and he had taken their money? He, the boy wonder, the paragon of Towerhill. He shut his eyes, screwing them tight and waited for the coup-de-grace. But it never came. The priest blessed himself and turned back to face the altar: 'Benedicat vos, omni potens deus, pater et filii, et spiritu sancti, Amen.'

He got another dig in the ribs from Willie Hogan: 'Wake up ya bleddy eejit, the mass is ended.' He turned to see the priest descending serenely from the altar. He jumped up, standing on the end of his soutane in his haste, almost pulling it from his shoulders and sheepishly followed into the sacristy.

He did not linger with the small groups of men who huddled in various corners of the village after mass. He was too afraid of exposure, although Father Cassidy, mysteriously, had kept his own counsel. He slipped quietly unseen, across the fields behind the church and was gone on the long road home well before the main bunch of worshippers.

*   *   *

'Had I youth's blood and hopeful mood, the heart of fire once more?' sang his father, 'for all the gold the earth might hold I'd never quit your shore.' Jimmy raked the garden grass as his father scythed and sang. He smiled a little and thought what a straightforward, uncomplicated man his father was, a man content in his time, sure of his place, a true lover of his country. It seemed easy to make him happy, a fine day, a good horse to ride, a few glasses of beer in the pub on Sunday. He never read much except the paper but he followed the news and politics avidly. 'Dev is the best bleddy man this country ever saw,' he often said. Just now he had finished telling Jimmy about the raid the Flying Column made on the Black and Tan Barracks in 1921 and Jimmy sighed as his father described again how the bullets had grazed the grass at his heels, as he and the great Charlie Hurley and John Lordan had pinned one hundred men of the best army in the world down for two hours before being forced to make a run for it, out the Laurel Walk, across the fields and away.

Because he had heard it so often, it always seemed an intolerable length of time to Jimmy before his father finally finished his stories of the time of, "the trouble." The burden of nationalism was an almighty heavy one. Jimmy much preferred Gunsmoke or Biff Bailey Fighting Fury. It was all so colourful and slick and up to date. His father's stories were old-fashioned, from another time and place. 'Why don't you read about Michael Collins?' his father would ask. The answer to that was simple. There were no comics about Irish history. It was all grey men in grey textbooks, losing grey, weary wars.

His father swung closer and closer to the oak tree. Jimmy tensed in alarm. In another second he would see the moss stuffing the hole where his precious box of comics was hidden. If his father only knew what treasures lay inside the hollow tree trunk. Worse still, if he found out how he acquired his latest edition of Tiger? A pang of guilt shot through his stomach and down his legs to his toes as if he were stabbed by an arrow.

'The tea is ready,' shouted his mother from the hall door.

'That's the best bleddy word all day,' said his father, laying the scythe against the tree. Saved again, thought Jimmy, and not a moment too soon.

"Live comfortlessly," was his mother's dictum, instilled in her no doubt by her ancestors: generations of hardworking Devon Protestants; only they had converted and become Catholics; more Irish than the Irish themselves. His father ate his food with pleasant, chewing sounds, enjoying every mouthful, while his mother stood at the table-end and nibbled at a piece of dry toast. She never sat at the table, always up and ready and providing. How could she have so much energy when she ate so little? To

Jimmy it was an eternal mystery. She was frugal as a Scotsman, his father joked. *'Pay what you owe,'* she would quote, *'and then you may go to the fair of Timahoe.'* Her passion for paying her debts was only surpassed by her love of poetry. Jimmy in turn got his literary streak from her. He sank his fork into a potato but could not look either of them in the eye. He would be a stranger to them if they ever discovered his crime.

For the next few days he felt like a person walking on eggs. On Tuesday the long journey home from school seemed interminable. On each bend of McCarthy's lane he expected to meet a stern-faced, vindictive Josie, looming tall, standing up in his rubber-wheeled cart, urging his fiery-nostrilled horse towards him: like the angel Gabriel in his burning chariot, sweeping sinners to hell. For Christ's sake, not even Buck Jones could help him now with two six-shooters full of lead, much less Roy of the Rovers. How stupid he had been, how self-indulgent.

He agonised over his arithmetic book on Wednesday as Master O'Donnell rolled a hardened gob of phlegm under his tongue and spat accurately into the flames of the wood fire. The flames hissed like snakes and licked higher. Master O'Donnell did this several times a day out of sheer exasperation from trying to drill learning into unreceptive heads. The children were more attuned to the demands of the land: milking cows, feeding pigs, drawing water from the well. Living in the midst of nature they could not easily appreciate the subtleties of higher maths, and so the poor man beat his head against a brick wall. 'My heart and my health,' he cried, sitting on a high stool and clawing at his thin, sandy hair like a demented heretic: 'my heart and my health is gone from ye. Day in, day out I say the same things and nothing ever sinks home...

scalded ... tormented...' He rambled on in a high, crazed monologue which the children long since knew by heart. Willie Hogan mouthed the words in syncopation behind his back while Jimmy and Mary Finnegan, with tremendous willpower, stifled their pent-up mirth. Jimmy clapped his hand over his mouth and coughed loudly but this only added to the silent hilarity welling up like fizzy champagne inside them. Finally Mary Finnegan could contain it no longer, and she exploded into gales of abandoned laughter that brought Master O'Donnell up short and quickly erased his torture. From cloying anguish he went to savage fury in the twinkling of an eye. 'What have you to be laughing at you brazen bitch?' he demanded, 'sure your brain is like a muddy pool that the ducks have just left. Get out that door! And you two: mister-know-alls, who know nothing, get out with her!' Mary scooted out gleefully followed by Jimmy and the sniggering Willie Hogan.

By Friday morning he felt better. The danger seemed past. He had met Josie on the lane on Thursday cutting the briar-filled fences with his scythe. Their conversation was as cheerful as ever: talk of football, the weather, the neighbours, crops, cows and bulls. So it was all the more joltingly shocking when Josie called after him as he rounded the farmyard on Friday evening on the last leg of his journey home: 'Jimmy, come here a minute.'

'Oh, hello Josie.'

'D'you remember that envelope I gave you last week to give to the priest?'

With a quickening heartbeat, drying mouth, a sinking feeling like staying too long on a swingboat, he turned to face Josie with a stupid smile frozen on his face. 'Oh yeah, I gave it to him.'

'But he only got nineteen shillings - I gave you a pound.'

Hooked like a salmon in the Bandon river, well and truly wriggling. 'Oh, I gave it ...ah, I mean...he got it alright - last Thursday - or maybe 'twas Friday.'

Josie was firm but not angry. Yet behind his eyes there lurked a major threat. 'I know he got it, boy,' he said, impatiently, 'Christ I know that. But 'twas the amount he got. Nineteen silver shillings instead of one green, paper pound. Now, how's that?'

'Well, I dunno ...at all...'

'Don't tell me lies,' interjected Josie firmly, ''tis bad enough breaking the pound besides telling me bleddy lies as well. Sure the priest himself told me. He wanted to know how I could manage only nineteen shillings - I mean the man was insulted. Can't blame him.'

Jimmy swallowed and wished the ground would swallow him. This was the end of his friendship with Josie and no mistake. He felt as if he were hurtling down Blackgate Hill with no brakes on his bicycle. 'I gave him the envelope alright, Josie,' he said desperately, trying to salvage something, some shred of dignity, some excuse where there was none: 'I gave him the money but I changed it in the shop first.'

'Christ you did, boy,' said Josie getting quite annoyed, 'and you kept a shilling into the bargain. How d'you think that makes me look to the bleddy priest?'

Then Jimmy realised that it wasn't the simple larceny that bothered Josie. It was the priest's opinion of him that mattered. Josie McCarthy, a strong farmer being so niggardly as to give the priest only nineteen shillings instead of a pound. It was only a trifle yet it denoted a whole attitude and a way of thinking. It was slightly parsimonious. It was shameful.

Suddenly it all dawned on Jimmy. He felt desperately sorry for what he had done to Josie, 'Jesus, I'm sorry Josie,' he blurted out. 'I took that shilling alright. I bought a comic with it.'

'Yerra, I don't care what you did with it, boy. If you asked me for a shilling I'd gladly give it to you. But that's not the point. 'Tis the stealing. And the priest will announce the dues from the altar. Everyone will know how much I gave - I'll be ruined.'

Crimers-a-war, thought Jimmy, 'tis worse than I thought: 'But you can tell 'im I ...I took it, like,' stuttered Jimmy. 'I mean you can blame me.'

'No need for me to blame you,' said Josie with a shrug. 'Sure didn't the priest himself tell me. He figured out how the money went astray.'

'He did?' exclaimed Jimmy in shock. That snaky, smiling Father Cassidy. Never pretended a bit. How could he face him on the altar next Sunday? He was finished as an acolyte. 'And you'll have to explain to your father,' added Josie, 'I had to tell him you know.' Jimmy's eyes widened until they bulged like sprouting potatoes: 'My father knows about it?' he gasped in despair. 'He bleddy does,' said Josie with finality as he turned away, 'and he's waiting for you at home this minute.' Josie turned on his heel and stepped smartly across the yard with that precise gait: slightly bow-legged, each foot smiting the ground firmly as his Wellington boots flapped at his calves with a lubba-lubba sound. Reeling, Jimmy could only stare after him.

So his father knew. His hands were tingling, his stomach churning, his face was hot. He drew in a deep breath, blew out his cheeks as he exhaled and struck for home in a whirlwind of emotion. As he walked the narrow path, beaten down from long usage across the last two fields to home, his thoughts went through a series of loops and dives. He was angry at Josie for catching him out, and then for telling his father. What kind of a friend was Josie? He could do no wrong in Josie's eyes until he had taken the shilling. But then the game changed. And Jimmy himself had broken the rules. His anger gave way to self-pity. Things were tough: walking to school in bare feet; milk and brown bread every day for lunch, the weary trudge home in the evening. Even the shortcut through Jordan's brake and Shorten's farm was scarcely a shortcut at all because by the time you had climbed over all those huge ditches from field to field, you felt as if you'd been in the Grand National. E.S.B had won it that year from the Queen of England's horse, Devon Loch, whose legs had seized up on the last hundred yards to the finish. Michael O'Hehir, the radio commentator almost had a seizure himself. Jimmy very definitely felt like Devon Loch today as he leaped from the last fence and trudged across the ploughed field, through the haggard and into the farmyard. He paused to collect his wits in preparation for the inevitable confrontation. Every sense was on edge like a razor. The leaves rustled in the slight north-east wind that blew from the gate going up the fields. A few Brown Leghorn and White Wynedot hens pecked at some oats his mother had scattered for them on the footpath. From the distant fields came the hum and grind of a threshing machine, probably Morleys or O'Haras harvesting the corn. The starlings swooped and dived in huge clusters overhead, arching, wheeling, constantly changing rhythm and formation in a miracle of precision aerodynamics. Normally he would regard them in fascination for long periods of time but this evening far weightier problems preoccupied him.

The dogs barked joyously upon seeing him, wagging their tails furiously and leaping up to lick his face, placing both paws on his shoulders. 'Down boys, down,' he said brushing them away as he entered the back door to the kitchen.

The grandfather clock tick-tocked loudly. The table had some clutter of cups and jars, baking soda and a tray. The fire embers burnt low and the heavy, black kettle hanging on the iron crane emitted occasional puffs of steam. He breathed a sigh of relief. Nobody home. A reprieve. Maybe Josie was only trying to teach him a lesson? Maybe he hadn't told his father? He threw down his school satchel and went out to the garden in front of the house. His mother was tending her beehives, dressed from head to toe in his father's clothes for protection from stings. Over her head she had a square, beekeeper's box hat, with a muslin cloth stretched tightly over her face. 'Anything to eat, Mam?' he called expectantly.

'Whisht,boy,' she replied, 'I'm in the middle of this. Hold on a minute.'

His mother hated cooking and would gladly spend all her time out of doors, walking, travelling, discovering. Perhaps it was her Adventurer's blood. That's what Master O'Donnell called the early Elizabethan settlers in the deep south-west. He smirked and turned back inside. He began to cut some slices of fresh, brown, soda bread when he heard a light tread on the doorstep. A shadow darkened the door: his father's shadow. Jimmy kept his back to him, munching the thick crust and mumbled: 'Mam's at the bees, I s'pose we'll have to wait for the grub.'

No reply. His father stood in the middle of the floor, silent, tight-lipped: a lithe, strong man, fair hair greying; not too tall, but imposing. The ticking of the clock seemed to becoming a deafening boom. Jimmy knew he was for it without turning around.

'Did you take Josie McCarthy's money?' demanded his father, voice quiet but icy.

'I did,' said Jimmy, quivering.

'And what the devil did you do that for?'

'To buy Tiger,' said Jimmy.

'To buy Tiger?' repeated his father incredulously, 'you mean that bloody English comic?'

Jimmy nodded.

'I thought I told you to get them foreign pieces of trash out of this house?'

Jimmy said nothing, staring, unable to speak.

'Answer me,' shouted his father, 'I told you not to draw my anger on you.'

'Twas the end of the story,' stuttered Jimmy, 'I wanted to know who won the soccer game...in Roy of the Rovers.'

'The curse of Cromwell on Roy of the Rovers,' roared his father, 'do you know what you're after doing? You've disgraced the bleddy family that's what you've done. Christ man, we were never beholden to the McCarthys, nor to the bleddy priest either. There was never any roguery or trickery in this house; and all because of a dirty English comic.'

'I'm sorry,' muttered Jimmy, 'I won't do it again.'

'That's not good enough my man,' exclaimed his father, 'you don't steal in this house, and you don't bring rotten English propaganda in here either. We kicked them out of here in '22, and you, you little fool are accepting all their ways again...after all our hardship.'

'Sure 'tis only about soccer,' cut in Jimmy innocently.

'Are you back-answering me?' demanded his father, towering over him, seeming to become a giant in his anger.

'No...no...I mean...' He searched for words to explain, to exonerate, but there were none. He was trapped like a bird in a cage. His mother appeared in the kitchen in the nick of time.

'Arthur,' she said to his father, 'aren't you taking all this too far. It's only a small thing.'

'Small things can become big things,' said his father.

'Let him go to Josie and apologise.'

'Apologise,' said his father, 'after what's been said? No, there will be no apologies, to Josie McCarthy of all people.'

'You know as well as I do that there is more to this than taking a shilling,' said his mother, 'your argument with Josie has been a long time coming, and if this hadn't started it something else would have.'

'What do you mean?' asked his father.

'I mean the Civil War, Arthur, Jimmy is too young to know about it.'

'He doesn't know and he doesn't care,' said his father.

'We all know and care,' said his mother, 'but you've got to stop looking back. The war is over.'

'It's not over yet by God,' said his father.

Abruptly his father moved to the window and stood gazing out at the green grass of the garden. Jimmy stole a furtive glance at him. The clock continued to tick. When his father turned back finally he was calm and controlled. 'I'm disappointed in you, Jimmy,' he said, 'for 'tis yourself you've let down most of all, 'tis yourself you've disgraced.'

His father turned on his heel and strode out the door. Jimmy looked at his mother who looked distressed and annoyed, but said nothing. Jimmy eventually heard the sound of horse hooves and went out into the yard. His father had saddled the chestnut gelding and was sitting tall in the saddle. As Jimmy appeared he touched the horse's flanks with his heels and trotted away out of the yard and up the fields without speaking or acknowledging Jimmy's presence. Jimmy followed, puzzled and fearful. What he did not know then but would discover later was that his father and Josie had a terrible row over the shilling. Rough words had been exchanged and threats of violence uttered. The simmering feud from the bad old days was revisited. Jimmy had inadvertently reopened wounds from the past. Terrible hurts from old battles and betrayals. But he was too young to know about it, like his mother said. He wandered through the fields in search of his father like a lost soul, fearing the worst. Had he started another civil war?

IN JASPER'S WOOD

It was the sweet summertime. There was a sound of water flowing, a sound of hacking, a song of a lark in clear air. The water was a shallow stream flowing across a flat bog towards a steep-sided gorge where the stream flew faster as it narrowed, plunging downwards. There was a broad-leaved oakwood with knarled trees growing on either steep slope of the gorge, and the trees were very old. Their branches spread out and up as if they would embrace and gather in and shelter all living things. And in the wood was birdsong, the plop of acorns falling, dogs' distant barking across the river. There was the swish of leaves and the crackle of twigs under the feet of squirrels and rabbits. Woodcock and pheasant came with curious eyes and throaty cries and pecked and bobbed in continuous motion. And sometimes there was the whoosh of wings as a sneaky weasel disturbed their nervous treading in the shadows.

There was a sound of bumble bees buzzing on honeysuckle boughs and a smell of sticky resin from the bark of pine trees; soft sunlight on bluebells in the clearings, an air of mystery and a fringe of ghosts in a large, old, walled estate just out of sight. And somewhere outside and beyond the walls and wood a sound of voices carried down. A hooded crow floated from the canopy of trees and followed upstream until it became wider and slower. On one side of the stream was a huge, grassy field that rose in gentle, rolling curves like waves upon a briny sea, and stretched away to where a road ran high above. Anyone standing on the road would have a panoramic view of wood and bog, and high brakes and uplands on the far side of the bog.

There was a lone man standing on the road in a cloth cap and a tweed suit. He smoked a pipe and he carried a slash-hook for cutting briars under his arm. He was tall and broad-shouldered and his eyes were set wide apart and cold and steady. He looked out upon his holding with the ruddy assurance of a man who had little to fear in his corner of the world. His name was Jasper Eustace and he owned a thousand acres of the ground beneath his feet. He saw the crow floating over bullrushes and long, bearded reeds with white, fluffy tips like feathers, like brooms; and over snowy bog cotton and blue violets and yellow buttercups, until it came to where two men were building a stone wall bordering the far side of the bog.

One of the men building was mature and beyond his prime: tall and angular with a strong nose and quite thick lips. His face was long and thin and the skin over his cheekbones was taut. His eyes were hooded, pale-blue and his forehead sloped backwards. From the side it was a sensitive face and could be handsome. The man was dressed in a black suit with an open-necked, white shirt. His body was lank and loose, emphasised all the more by his long, elegant arms and longer tapering fingers. He wore a felt hat which he would remove now and again, wiping his sweating brow, then settling it back on his head. He removed his jacket and placed it on the wall.

'Tis hot,' said the younger man.

'It is faith,' said the older man. He knelt and rolled a large boulder into position at the base of the wall. Although the stone was heavy and unwieldy he manoeuvred it with ease and dexterity, as if the stone were lighter than it appeared; as if the stone were doing half the work for him, doing his bidding. The way he touched it was almost a caress and in return the stone was happy to yield, as if alive and responsive to an artist's understanding. He carried on rising the wall hour upon hour, stone upon stone, calmly and unhurried, so that from morning the wall had grown and stretched long and elegant through the day. A thing of beauty, as if moulded by nature's wind, sand, water over a million years. And the man's personality reflected and echoed the wall: graceful, centred, impregnable, gentle. The younger man, though eager and impatient at the start, had learned by evening to watch the older man and temper his enthusiasm and take advice: 'You must let the stone do the work, Sonny boy.' The young man laughed ruefully and held out his blistered hands. 'You're right, John James,' he agreed and did not need to say more. The older man moved his head with a slow, repeated motion: 'The stones will best you in the long run. You must humour them; take your time. Life is long but a stone's life is longer than a man's; and tomorrow is another day.'

The younger man nodded. He'd learned to listen. He was little more than a youth of eighteen. He had an open, slightly pale face, with a fair complexion and even features, and he looked upon the world without rancour and also without fear. He had on a shirt, waistcoat and a thick, wide, frieze pants. His movements were graceful and unhurried and his body inside the loose clothes was wound like a spring, a jackknife. He was broad of shoulder and taller than he looked, though not as tall as the older man. His eyes were twinkling, smiling, summer-blue, but they could become cold, killer's eyes with winter in the iris. But they were not yet, and had not been called to kill. The older man was John James O'Grady of the townland where they worked, and the younger, Sonny Hayes: a neighbouring farmer's son from up the road.

The stream emerged from the wood and ran on through copses, and under bridges until it reached flat, wide fields and another river flowing eastwards to the sea. At the confusion of the two rivers a wider river formed and flowed on until it dissected the ancient, crumbling town of Bandon, and in a tavern in the town were soldiers getting restless from the heat and choleric from drinking whiskey. The more they drank the louder they became and they were looking for some bait to draw their anger. Their leader was a mean English captain named Howard, who had fought in the Great War and who had the blood of many people on his hands. He wore a uniform of black tunic and tan trousers and he and his cohorts were called, the "Black and Tans" by the locals. He drained the last of his whiskey and stood up and growled, 'Let's go shoot some pork.'

Then, as an afterthought he leant in over the bar with a swoop of his hand and his fingers clutched the neck of a whiskey bottle like the talons of a kestrel clutching prey. At the same time he kept his eyes, cold and level on the bar-owner, gauging his response. The owner quickly lowered his gaze and did not move or utter one protest. Howard gave a sneer at the man's timidity and waved the bottle towards his band of desperadoes.

They swaggered out, insolent cigarettes dangling from the corners of their mouths, and muscled old men, women and children into the dusty street off the footpath. They crossed the street called, South Main, and clambered noisily into a Crossley Tender lorry that had a flat-bed and high sides with mesh wire resembling a cage. In the enclosed, snub-nosed cab in front, the driver and Howard sat. They slowly moved down the narrow street, past shops with names carved over the doors. The names fell on the tongue with an Anglo-Saxon resonance: Lee, Good, Chinery, Sweetnam. There were farmers driving horses and carts and other townsfolk on bicycles and on foot. Most of the people lowered their eyes and did not salute the soldiers or acknowledge them in any way, and to a disinterested onlooker they might have been moving in a parallel universe, such was the gulf of hostility and indifference that lay between them. Even the well-dressed businessmen with trilby hats averted their gazes.

The lorry turned left past a Methodist church with long, elegant, arched windows and crossed a solid, granite bridge with seven buttressed arches. Up along the river the sun dazzled on a weir of white water where busy ducks harvested for minnows and other scraps. The ducks had their beaks in the river depths and backsides turned tail-up into the blue afternoon, as if they alone had the temerity to insult these interlopers to the tranquil town in as crude a manner as any the soldiers could contrive. At the bridge-end the Masonic Hall stood imposing and implacable; and opposite, the statue of the Maid of Erin was a silent cenotaph to a more innocent Gaelic past. The town straggled up Kilbrogan Hill where some dubious solicitors plied their arcane trade, hidden from the suspicious eyes of townspeople in a terrace of rather graceful, four-storey Georgian houses. Across the street was the entrance to the military barracks, a grim fortress out of which the soldiers only ventured in the bright light of day, aided and abetted by their civilian counterparts in the Royal Irish Constabulary. As the hill went higher the lorry traversed a wide, open area dominated by a round, stone building called the Shambles, within who's cyclopean walls cheerful butchers had slaughtered cattle and pigs for consumption by the townspeople for many a hundred year. And continued to do so; oblivious to the faint, sweet smell of blood and entrails, and the blood-spattered patterns on the floor and walls.

The town had formed on either side of a deep recess cut out by the surging river. On the near side a tall-spired Protestant church rose up against Kilbrogan Hill. On the opposite hill sat two further churches. One was Catholic with a plain, square tower that seemed too high for its flanking transepts and nave, giving it the appearance of having a large head and a stumpy body. Yet another Protestant church bestrode an elevated site called Gallows Hill: a name that encompassed a grim history: many a croppy boy, with scalp blackened from tar and feathers, had dangled there at the end of a rope after various failed rebellions to which the native Irish were serially addicted.

Soon the Tans were going west along the banks of the Bandon river, along the rutted, dusty road, passing the whiskey bottle from hand to hand like an unholy grail. They drank the liquour with greedy, noisy slurps and wiped their sullen lips, swaying against each other when the lorry rolled drunkenly over potholes. And they took comfort from the body heat and musky smells and fleeting eye contact. But what gave them most comfort was the assurance of their fingers on the triggers of their rifles; and these fingers constantly moved, caressing the triggers, the way a child would caress a chestnut or the smooth bannister of a stairs. Because behind their crude bravado lurked a gnawing fear. They had fear even as they played God with their Lee Enfields and Webleys and bayonets. They feared the myriad winding roads and the chill mists on sudden hills. And the cold rain which could quickly change the complexion of the brightest summer's day. They feared the colder Irish who could also charm and seduce, and who had been here six thousand years. Who had grown accustomed to hard rain and dry wind; who could sleep in rough habitats with cold comforts, and endure weeks of no sunlight. Who survived blight and famine. Who were poets and could be killer angels. Who mythologised the death of suns, the cry of curlews, who loved horses; who stood stones to their dead and whose dead became the stones, standing guard over the living in the winter solstice. The Tans feared the unknowable, they feared the brave and the cunning, and the gunmen in the night. And the way a leafy summer wood could become a deathtrap of blood and screaming, when these strange-sounding natives ambushed them without warning in the middle of a cloudless afternoon.

They had learned to be wary at all times and in all seasons, because this was a new and treacherous confrontation into which they had been thrust as reluctant conscripts. Their officers, the Auxiliaries, like Howard, knew the hell of the trenches of France in the Great War just finished: men who knew no other way to live. Battle-hardened, hard-hearted, they were sent to Ireland to put down an incipient rebellion that looked like it might get out of hand. But many of the ordinary soldiers, the Tans, were prisoners and criminals on parole from the jails of England. Theirs was Hobson's choice. And they wondered which was better: the passage to a mouldering prison cell in Dartmoor or the uneasy dicing with death played with shadowy figures in an alien land.

In the Hayes household, Sonny's eldest sister, Elizabeth was hurrying to finish baking a brown soda cake, because she was conscious that the men liked tea in the fields at four in the afternoon. Sonny always said food tasted better out of doors and John James liked a regular schedule on the days he was helping out the Hayes family. He had a small-holding himself of twenty acres and this meant he only worked part-time. He'd always start at eight in the morning and come back for the dinner at midday when the fare usually consisted of floury potatoes, cabbage or turnips, bacon and gravy. It was always fish on Fridays but something like steak or beef was a rarity reserved for Sundays. At four in the afternoon he liked a break for tea and he was always gone by six on the dot. Elizabeth kept snatching glances at the grandfather clock as it tick-tocked towards the hour. She was on her own today, like many days now that the younger girls were gone. Because their mother had died with the youngest in childbirth Elizabeth bore a heavy burden as surrogate. She'd held things together for six long years until she could no longer take the strain. Her father, Joseph, was getting on in years and, having sired fourteen children, he considered that the world owed him a certain amount of leisure time, which he usually passed in the local public house. She'd reared the young ones in direst poverty. A kindly neighbour's wife with a baby of her own had come daily to suckle young baby, Hannah. The kindness of strangers. But Elizabeth had to run the household, grow up before her time. The banks were pressing and evicted them. They had to leave the farm in the dead of winter and travel by a horse and cart, forty miles, to lodge temporarily in a farmhouse with no roof. Sonny had caught pneumonia as a boy of nine. She had to use all her craft and powers of persuasion to recover the farm. Then the little girls were swept out of her sight by a cousin priest, to the Black Country coal fields of England and a new life, with their masses of golden hair, their freckles and trusting smiles; to start again with strangers, with strange creeds, customs and language. To Elizabeth their departure was a great disaster but she felt relief because they were fed at least, clothed at least. To her mother it would have been an unforgettable wound. To her father it was anaesthetised by whiskey.

Elizabeth was a tall, dark-haired girl with a sculpted jaw-line and dark, dancing eyes which always carried the hint of a smile. She moved with an easy grace and was considered the best-looking girl in that part of the country. Now twenty-eight, she was the eldest. Two brothers, William and John were long gone to Boston and New South Wales. There were other brothers scattered about the place: Michael, volatile, talented, breaking horses, gone riding across the neighbouring farms, clearing ditches as he went. Wild in the blood. There was Richie, a cattle-dealer, tangling in ponies, sheep, pigs: anything with four legs. There was Joe, the phlegmatic one; and Sonny: smiling, warm, and true.

The baking cake was in a round, black bastible hanging on a crane over an open turf fire. She'd lift the cover every so often and give the cake a gentle prod with a fork. It was rising nicely and turning a rich, nut-brown colour. She hoped she hadn't added too much bread soda, which was good for rising but could cause heartburn. The kitchen was filled with the pleasant, sweet aroma caused by the raisins interacting with the flour, and the smoky smell of the burning turf. She went to the window and took stock of the day's complexion. The weather was holding.

There was a panoramic view in three directions from where the farmhouse stood on a high plateau, ten miles from the sea. To the south-west was Corrin Hill and from that point a ridge ran parallel with the coastline, south-east to Kinsale. In between the farm and the distant ridge lay the lush valley of the Bandon fed by tributary rivers such as the Belrose and the Ballafola, with the twin villages of Enniskean and Ballineen along the riverbank. Westward the rainy town of Dunmanway huddled under the Sheha Mountains.

All along the riverbank were substantial farms occupied in large part by better-off families with names like Bateman, Jennings, Hosford, Eustace. The further away from the river you travelled the smaller the holdings became and the poorer the soil. The folk subsisting in these uplands were McCarthys, Murphys, O'Mahonys, O'Donovans, Hurleys: names of the old Gaelic chieftains who were driven out, burnt out after the Battle of Kinsale in the year 1601. The greatest of them, O'Sullivan Beare, gone north to Breffni in the dead of winter, over many a river bridged with ice and many a vale with snowdrifts dumb. Carrying the remnants of his clan on the long march with cloak and shield. Attacked on every side. One thousand reduced to thirty-five warriors and only one woman. The ghostly remnant of a great nation, gone north into the dark forever. The day the great

Gaelic-speaking nation died. Defeated and banished by Elizabethan adventurers led by Mountjoy and Carew.

These invaders had brought with them their work ethic, their dour, puritan religion, their grim tenacity. And of course their language. Gradually the poetic, sibilant Gaelic sounds were replaced by the harsher, clipped English. But they also brought their love of husbandry, their appreciation of order and beauty, their love of trees, hedgerows, gardens and wildlife. And their own pecking order and class distinctions.

On the lower rungs of the social ladder were the bag-carriers, who, as meagre reward after Kinsale's rout had been parcelled out small-holdings on rougher ground and who scrabbled for the same allotments as the displaced Irish. These were Shortens, Chambers, Pattersons, Whelpleys, Deans. The poorest of the poor were the landless Catholic peasants who survived in cottages of stone, slate and thatch, some still mud-walled and whose numbers had been devastated in the Great Famine of 1847: who had died in millions from starvation and on coffin ships bound for America. At the top of the totem pole, Lord Bandon held sway in a grand Gothic pile of granite on a prominent lookout over the river. Away from the house, stands of oak, beech, hazel and willow stretched across thousands of undulating acres of grassland and wildflower meadows, where cattle and horses grazed in grass to the knee. Lord Bandon extracted rents and tithes from many small-holders in a line due west to Dunmanway, regardless of creed or country of origin.

But the proud Irish never forgave or forgot their displacement and wanted an independent nation once again. They resented paying ground rents to absentee landlords like Bandon who lived in England and rarely set foot on Irish soil. Some had stronger titles than others: fee farm grants, leases for lives renewable forever, leases for five hundred years, assignments, sub-leases. The odd squireen like Jasper Eustace had a fee simple, which made him independent of Bandon's grasp. All documents of conveyance were drafted in dusty offices by those bronchial, money-grubbing solicitors and scriveners who, even though most were Catholic, had no intention of severing the link either with Bandon or the Crown. Many of the large shopkeepers, bankers, farmers and clergy of either stripe, were in the same boat. All fed from the same communal trough. But conversely, some of the lowly planters wavered in between loyalty to the Crown and the advantages a country of their own governance would bring. And now, a dark wind was blowing since the leaders of the 1916 Rebellion in Dublin had been brutally shot by firing squad. And deep, red, fire embers, which threatened a conflagration, were burning in men's hearts.

Elizabeth could see the tops of the trees in Jasper's Wood in her peripheral vision on the left. Straight ahead were the wide fields of green, growing corn, wheat and barley, that again thinned out as the ridge rose on the south side of the Bandon where land met sky. Just beyond the horizon was the broad Atlantic. From some parts of the farm you could see the azure-blue ocean that always filled Elizabeth with an explicable longing. For what she wasn't sure. A wider world perhaps? A foreign shore? Perhaps to follow her brother, William, to the woods of Massachusetts, or John to the outback of Australia. To see her little sisters once again. To hold their hands and hear their joyful laughter. And yet her centre lay within these larksong fields, these white roads to western Sheha, these singing groves of starlings. She loved the comforting bark of dogs on the hills at night. She remembered her mother whose bones lay in the local churchyard and whose face rose before her in her dreams. She was happy here.

She took the cake out of the bastible and placed it to cool on a tray on the solid beechwood table. She hoped it wasn't too fresh for John James, but she knew he'd like the raisins. She cut a number of slices from the hot cake and smeared butter on them with a knife. The butter quickly melted. She wrapped the bread in newspaper and put the package in a string shopping-bag where she'd already placed a flask of sweet, hot tea. Then she went out the back door into the farmyard.

A slated, stone building with stall and loft stood at right angles to the house, and across the wide yard was a long, low outhouse that now housed pigs, cattle, a stables for the horses and a car-house for the trap and common car. This was a former dwelling, Elizabeth herself had been born there, and several of the older brothers. A previous generation of fourteen children had been raised there, had grown, taken wing, and vanished. Before that previous generations. She sometimes felt there were ghosts in every corner, behind every whispering elm tree, looking over every gate. Her bicycle leant against the house gable and she slung the shopping-bag over the handlebars. Because it was a downhill run all the way to the bog she'd be there in ten minutes. Two barking collies raced her all the way.

Father Jerome Casey had completed his ministrations in the local church in the village of Ballycummin. He'd said the Mass, possibly a little hastily because it was a weekday and his congregation was small, just the daily communicants. He'd prayed novenas for the dead and had cleaned and polished golden chalice and silver thurible. He'd defrocked and neatly folded his long, white cassock, silk rope with the tassels, chasuble and stole: the ornate garments of his calling. He'd read his office from his breviary and finished his breakfast in the fine parish house he occupied with his housekeeper, Mrs. Lordan. And it was still only twelve o'clock in the day, such a lovely day. He had one sick call to make on the road to Enniskean and after that he was minded to go on one of his occasional walks through the woods, which he liked to do when a fine day stretched before him. 'I think I'll take the afternoon off, Brigid,' he said, 'while the day is fine.'

'Do father,' replied Mrs Lordan, like a satisfied hen, 'it's a glorious day, thank God.'

'A day for the open road and the woods and streams,' he said.

'Off you go and forget your responsibilities for a few hours.'

'I think I will,' he repeated.

'The very thing,' added Mrs Lordan with a hint of smugness. Because in his absence she'd have the run of the presbytery and could shape it to her satisfaction. She'd polish and sweep and wash without interruption or any tiresome interjections from the priest. She liked order, minutiae. Above all no dust or dirt. She liked things spartan. That's how she used to keep her own childless house until her husband died, and she moved in permanently to care for Fr. Casey. And he could be untidy. Slovenly even, dare she say it. A constant, firm hand was needed to keep things right. A man needed a maid. But she of course held no such lowly post. She was a priest's housekeeper, with power behind the throne.

Father Casey walked down the tree-lined avenue from the presbytery with a spring in his step and a clear mind. Fulfilling your functions early in the day brought clarity of thought, ease, an uplift of the spirit. Behind him the house hulked square and solid with bay, Edwardian windows and a canopied roof adorned with red tiles. An imposing construction but not classical or beautiful. But what of that? It was the house of a gentleman. He pulled the double oak gates behind him, and tied the hinged metal hasp and shooting bolt to keep wandering cows out of his green lawns. He struck westward. The road wound a little higher past a labourer's cottage and then swung sharply down. Although he walked this stretch of road most days, the view from this high eminence always took his breath away. A blue mountain range stood on the western horizon and although Father Casey had never seen the Rockies this is how he imagined them to be. In between was a vast, vaulting sky with white, bundled clouds, moving imperceptibly in the lazy, summer breeze. Near him, green fields fell away on either side, rolling with the rivers down to the valleys below. A land falling and rising. Hollows and foothills, effulgent with ash and silver birch and sycamore; higher brakes bursting with yellow furze and fern. Up to the blue mountains: round-topped Sheha, Nowen like a pyramid; to the north, the Paps, like mammary glands. And dreamily, dim, distant: Macgillicuddy's Reeks, guarding the kingdom of Kerry. Father Casey felt good to be alive in such a place, on such a day as this.

The smell of new-mown hay filled his nostrils. Far off, the clatter of a mowing machine, a man following two strong Irish draughts: red, iron seat, green wheels, single beech-shaft lashed to collar and hames, the two horses pulling as one. The swathes of ripe hay laying down behind them and startled corncrakes scurrying to the safety of ditches full of brambles, ladyfinger, chickweed. The priest saluted two men cutting around headlands with scythes: swish, swish: 'God bless the work, Jimmy, Micheál.'

'That's a lovely day Father, thanks be to God,' in reply.

But no lingering. Familiarity outside of the circumscribed rituals of mass, station, funeral or wedding was not the done thing. Catholics had a pecking order too.

He heard the cuckoo as he left the mowers behind and he would await the corncrake's grating call as he returned at eventide for vespers. He saw a kestrel hovering as if suspended by an invisible line: grey-blue head and tail, red-brown upper parts, spotted with black: raptor on the wing, a small redpoll or goldfinch in its sights. Death unheralded in a golden afternoon. He was a great reader of the poems of Thomas Hardy and one always came to mind as he took his constitutional: *'When I set out for Lyonesse, a hundred miles away...'*

Ah, yes, he believed in God with a good deal more fervour on such a day as this. He gloried in dappled things, like Hopkins. Indeed it had been acknowledged in the seminary of Maynooth in his early days that he had quite a gift for verse, benignly approved of by the powers-that-be in mother church. But an overindulgence in artistic directions was not necessarily the best thing for a priest. A high moral code was required; art might lead on to licentiousness, heaven forfend.

Elizabeth was freewheeling down the shady lane towards Jasper's Wood crossroads, when the gun-metal grey Crossley Tender came around the corner of the Big Rock, three hundred yards away. On it came, tooting its horn, with the sound of raucous voices rising higher. She stopped in the middle of the four roads, put one foot on the ground and left the other on the pedal. She looked to her left and in the distance across the bog she saw her brother standing, while John James, bowed down, still worked on the wall. Who she did not see, but who saw her, was Father Casey hidden among a bunch of willows, where he had come to examine a phenomenon of nature in these parts: the imprint of a man's boot, a horse's hoof, the cut of a whip emblazoned on a flat, sandstone rock, about the size of a kitchen table. It was widely held among the locals to be a holy spot from where a priest, in the days of the penal laws, escaped from marauding yeomen. Was it an act of God or nature, or of man? Whatever the explanation, it was there for all to see, and a point of pilgrimage for many miles around.

Father Casey also saw the Black and Tans and pushed further into the willows out of sight. On the road, the quieter black and white collie stopped behind Elizabeth, perked up his ears and whined at the sound of the approaching lorry. The mottled-brown leading dog was already bounding across the bog to the two men. He stopped suddenly, sniffed the breeze and cocked his ears. He trembled and then shot off back, barking furiously. Sonny looked up from his work. He saw Elizabeth, then the lorry. He was conscious of his mouth going dry and a knot forming in his stomach: 'John James,' he whispered, 'the Tans.'

John James dropped his trowel, and slowly stood up, wiping the earth off his hands on the flanks of his trousers. He looked towards where Sonny pointed. He drew the back of his hand across his mouth. His face grew pale. They both stood, half-crouched in the lee of the stone wall. They saw the lorry stopping and Howard getting out of the cab.

Elizabeth stayed in the position she was already in with one foot on the pedal. As Howard came towards her she stood off the bicycle and held it in front of her. But if she was afraid she did not show it. She noticed his wide-set, expressionless eyes, prominent nose, heavy lips; high cheekbones, high forehead. A wide, beefeating face, with a scar slashed down the right cheek. He came on with a lugubrious walk, a revolver in a holster strapped on either thigh. The brown dog had reached them still barking. Elizabeth shushed it and it stood trembling and whining behind her with the other dog.

'Good afternoon,' smiled Howard, but the smile did not reach his eyes. Elizabeth said nothing. Howard said, 'Where's a fine young filly like you off to then?' She did not reply.

'No tongue, eh, what's in the bag?' He looked roughly inside. 'Going for a picnic, are we?'

Elizabeth was undecided whether to let her mission be known. Fearful of what might befall the two men, she said nothing.

'Any chance of some tea for the rest of us?' asked Howard, throwing an arm towards his drunken rabble. 'Maybe she'll take us home with her, sir,' shouted a voice from the flat-bed. Howard smiled grimly and walked around behind Elizabeth, getting an eyeful of her sensuous haunches outlined beneath her light, cotton dress. He leant in close to her swelling bosom and tumbling hair. 'How's about that then?' he drawled 'how's about taking us all for a picnic?' More guffaws from the back of the lorry. Elizabeth could feel his whiskey breath, hot on the back of her neck. He put his hand on her shoulders and thus caressing her he pulled her around to face him. He put a hand on her breast. She slapped him as hard as she could. Howard staggered back in shock with his hand up to his nose. Blood trickled through his fingers.

He pulled his hand away from his nose and looked down at the blood, examining it in detail. There was a deathly silence until Howard whispered, 'You'll pay for that.'

The dogs started up barking in clamorous unison. 'Shoot them,' he roared. Two soldiers jumped down and trained their rifles on the furious dogs. Two shots rang out and the dogs toppled over with wailing yelps. The brown one, still alive, shivered and whined, struggling to rise. Another bullet finished it off.

Inside the willow wood Father Casey blessed himself and crouched lower, clutching the willow bark until his knuckles whitened. He hated his cowardice but his fear of bullets was stronger than his self-loathing. He prostrated himself on the holy slab.

A man who could shoot a dog like that was not a man to be crossed. Elizabeth dropped the bicycle, and the teapot clattered on the road. The tea spilled out and made a looping pool across the dust. She ran as fast as she could towards the men in the bog. They were running towards, her oblivious to their own safety now. Despite his age, John James appeared the stronger and outran Sonny. He held a spade in his right hand. Howard lumbered down the road shouting to his soldiers. Like a hungry pack of beagles the soldiers grabbed up Elizabeth who kicked and screamed to no avail. Howard had only one objective and he was going to get his way. Four soldiers held Elizabeth, one on each limb. They arched her back and her summer dress was well above her spread knees, exposing the white softness of her inner thighs, the inviting darkness of her centre. Her wild struggling and screaming only made them more aroused.

But the world was suddenly fractured as things happened in a whirl. Into the churning mass of arms and legs, John James crashed the blade of the spade against the poll of one of the holding soldiers. The soldier moaned and fell with blood pumping. Possessed of strength of stone John James was swinging again when a second soldier stuck him in the gut with a bayonet, and the wind went out of him like the hiss of a stuck pig. Elizabeth was released as a different lust possessed the soldiers. Lust for blood. They fell on the prone John James in a frenzy of stabbing, that went on and on. If John James knew what had happened he quickly forgot, and his ending was swift as the death of a fox destroyed by hounds. He may have seen white lights and heaven beckoning. Maybe an angel held his hand and told him he was brave. Stone-mason welcomed home: man of rock returning.

Elizabeth ran to Sonny who held her close. She hid her face in horror. Sonny stood fully expecting the fate of John James to overtake him. Soldiers with bayonets pointed surrounded them on every side. Waiting for the word. Time ticked busy in the stillness.

But something had overcome Howard. An evening tristesse fell over his face. He felt detached, no longer supercharged, no longer out for blood and vengeance. Sufficient for today. The power was still his. He would conserve his energy for some future armageddon. He felt these people had the power too. And how could he contain it? They were not afraid of him despite his overwhelming arms: this girl, this boy. He saw it in their faces. He was tired of blood today. The body of John James lay inert and ragged on the road. The soldiers, shocked from killing, were expectant but waited for Howard to take command. They felt it in their hearts, their sober hearts. And knew they'd gone too far.

'Look to him,' said Howard, pointing to his cracked-skulled

underling who was wounded but not dead. He spun on his heel and strode towards the truck. The soldiers followed, holding their comrade between them. They reached the Crossley, and Howard said load up. The lorry went east along the road and climbed to the higher road where Jasper Eustace had been standing. Was still standing. Had seen all. Sonny and Elizabeth followed the trail of the departing lorry with their eyes. Saw it stop and saw words exchanged with their neighbour dressed in tweeds. Saw soldiers' respectful salutes and then pass on. And Jasper Eustace turned for home to his walled estate, his peacocks with spread tail-feathers, his stirrup cups, his hounds and horses. And washed his hands in a stream along the way, because all this did not concern him.

Father Casey crawled from his hiding place and hurried towards the bloody scene. Beads of sweat stood out on his brow. If Elizabeth and Sonny wondered where he came from they did not ask. He fumbled for his rosary beads and prayerbook, and put the stole he always carried, around his neck. And whispered in the dead man's ear, '*Oh, my God I am heartily sorry for having offended thee, and I detest my sins above every other evil…*

The gloaming was coming fast. Light was changing. Red clouds, orange clouds flooded the sky. Grey cumulus clouds underneath moved east, lighter mackerel overhead moved west. Still higher wisps of silver cloud moved north. The sun's burning rays diffused through all this colour were like the stairs to heaven. A shaft of rose-red light shone through a grove of trees and intersected the altar and cap stones of a stone circle. Sparrow hawks and peregrines floated above. Ospreys on wide, fingered wings came in from the sea.

AUBURN

On the highways of wide America, you can meet strange people; people of unexpected outlook and strange perception. I've recently been doing some travelling with my friend, Jane, and this particular Sunday in April we drove down the western slopes of the High Sierras in California, heading vaguely for some town in the Gold Rush country. The snow was thick at eight thousand feet, piled high on the roadside and cut straight down neatly at the edges by snowploughs. The wind shrieked up from plunging valleys, swirling in a frightening vortex at the mouth of the pass, buffeting our little car about like a match box.

'That's a fairy wind,' said Jane, as I was about to stop to admire the awesome view.

'It's nothing,' I said, as I slowed and stopped on the edge of a teetering precipice.

'Don't get out,' she said urgently, 'or you'll never be heard of again; the wind will take you.'

I shot her a disbelieving glance but the look in her eye said she meant it. Now Jane is only a slip of a girl, and young but she's wise as the devil, and tough as nails. She fools around a lot, playing pool and stuff, but when she's serious don't cross her. She's also got a kind of sixth sense, a power. You can see it in her eyes sometimes, maybe when she's looking at a sunset through cottonwoods, or leaning over a bridge watching a torrent of mountain water bursting downhill. She had that look in her eyes now. I revved the engine, heading down and west. Great stretches of pines and redwoods stood up against the sides of the peaks, climbing between blankets of snow. Near the summits where the bare rock emerged, the noble trees were reduced to withered wrecks, their scrawny branches, blasted and bare; many of their long trunks keeling over, lying flat and dead. They looked like a platoon of dead soldiers that charged a position in a battle, only to be repelled, broken and devastated, by the defenders. I pointed this out to Jane, and she marvelled at the likeness.

'D'you remember Picnic at Hanging Rock?' she asked.

'Oh yes, where the young girls disappear climbing a mountain in Australia.'

'Out of the blue, they were never heard of again. That would have been you back there if you'd gotten out of the car.'

I felt a cold chill on my spine. We left the highway and traversed the lower ranges, on a twisting back road as remote as a *boreen* in the west of Ireland. In Auburn, to where we at last descended, there were cowboys in chaps and tasselled jackets and big six-shooters on their hips, riding motor-cycles instead of horses. Here were verandas and boardwalks and false fronts like in Western movies. There was an old fire station painted maroon and white, housing an old, blackened fire engine. Around the sandy floor, thousands of copper pennies were scattered by passing tourists eager for good fortune or a good luck charm, as though by tossing a penny they could reach back to a safer, more certain past and so be buttressed against the vicissitudes and uncertainties of modern America. An enormous statue of Claude Chana stood on the spot where that trusty adventurer had first found the gold that started the mad rush westwards in the days of '49.

We picked up a hitch-hiker west of Donner Pass. He stood on the open highway carrying a red gasoline can, waving his thumb frantically.

'The poor fellow is stranded,' said Jane.

We took pity on him. He was a dark-haired, moustachioed fellow of about 30, powerfully built and ruddily handsome. He clambered in and settled himself in the back seat: 'Saved my bacon,' he panted.

'Have you been standing there long?' I asked.

'No, as a matter of fact, been real lucky; standing there not ten minutes.'

He settled himself in the back seat as if sitting on his own front porch.

'How far are you going?' asked Jane.

'I got my truck parked about a hundred miles south of here,' he said.

'A long way to take a can full of gas,' I said.

'Hell, this here can's my suitcase. No gas in here, see.'

He turned the can sideways to reveal a hole large enough for a hand. 'Just my pyjamas, and toothbrush and such.'

'That's a mighty clever thing,' said Jane in genuine admiration as a huge grin creased her girlish face. Jane gets uncommonly impressed at things at times. Clever I thought, but it made me uncomfortable being taken in.

'So you're a trucker,' repeated Jane, taken with the fellow.

'Yep,' he said, 'me and my pardner, we drive all over, from Florida to California. Oh yeah, it's a good life. My pardner, he takes care of business details, I take care of the loadin' an' drivin.'

'I read an article about trucking somewhere,' I began, 'it seems a tension-filled life.'

'Yeah, it's a very unstable life,' he said eager to talk, 'I mean, you pull into any truck stop, you always hear a guy on the phone yellin' an' screamin' 'cos his wife's carryin' on with some other guy back home. Most truckers support two families, always payin' for somethin; can't save any money.'

'Is that why they do drugs?' asked Jane.

'Some do,' he replied, 'but it ain't smart. I don't do drugs. Me and my pardner, we stay away from that stuff, then the cops don't bother ya. But you can find anything you want in a truck stop: girls, drugs, booze, you get it all on the C.B.'

I recalled a night I pulled into a truck stop, somewhere on the flat San Joaquin valley near Stockton; all these giant trucks lined up in a huge parking lot with their engines running. Eerie, no one around, dim lights from the street, papers blowing in the wind and the slow, deep, dangerous purr of the engines. They seemed alive and ready to pounce or maybe charge in a line across the compound like some deranged robots on wheels.

'Me and my pardner don't have any place we call home,' the man with the cannister continued wistfully, 'just the truck; a bed in the truck.'

'Would you like to have a home?' asked Jane, bless her warm heart.

'Oh, I'm gonna get me a wife,' he said, but not from America, an Indian wife, or maybe Filipino.'

'Why Filipino?'

'So's she can come here an' get a green card. I'm gonna advertise in the paper, or maybe go to the Phillipines in the fall.'

'So you like Oriental women?'

'I like all women. but this one's gotta be a physician.'

'A physician, no less?'

'They earn so much money, oh yeah. I can only save maybe two hundred bucks a week after payin' for everything; but physicians, they just clean up.'

'And what will you do then?'

'Me an' her, we'll build a house, and we'll have a garden, and four kids. Horses too, I like horses.' He had a faraway look in his eye.

'Essex, Montana way up near Glacier National Park, that's where we'll build it.'

Jane was intrigued and said: 'What if she doesn't like America?'

'Like it?' he said, 'she'll love it. Why wouldn't she?'

'Have you ever been in any other country?' I asked.

'Nope; wouldn't want to either. Can't imagine livin' anywhere but right here in the USA. Can't imagine her wantin' to be anywhere else either.'

Jane found this character intensely interesting and I must confess to being intrigued myself. But he wasn't all of a piece. Every few sentences he seemed to contradict himself.

'You know, my pardner has a plan,' he continued, 'to trap

animals: raccoons and foxes, in upstate New York or lately he's
been thinkin' 'bout Georgia.'

'For what?' asked Jane.

'To sell the skins, make money. He wants to give up the
truckin' business; too tough. Can't say as I agree with killing
animals though. I have a hard time with that. Killing animals for
your own gain. It's against God's plan.' He mumbled to himself
and looked out at the undulating valleys of the Motherlode
flashing by. I felt he had a screw loose.

'So you're going to get the physician?' repeated Jane, with a
twinkle in her eye.

'What I really wanna do,' he said, 'is travel round the world in
a boat, continent to continent, me and my old lady, maybe when
we're old and grey.'

He sighed and the faraway look returned. He didn't look like
someone who would ever stop wandering. There would always be
a reason to move on, to check out new horizons, follow a star.

'You folks are nice,' he said suddenly, 'where you folks from?'

'Ireland, but we live in San Francisco now,' we said.

'Really,' he exclaimed, 'I hadn't thought of Ireland.'

'You should look for an Irish wife,' said Jane, 'they're good
workers.'

'That's what I heard. Matter of fact my old Grandma on my
mother's side, she hailed from over there in Ireland, down
Cornwall way somewhere.'

Then he changed the subject again before we could respond:
'Ever heard of Dale Carnegie?'

'Sure.'

'How to win friends and influence people, my bible; you see I'm
a great listener.' Could have fooled me.

'Did you see the Killing Fields?' he continued.

'Yes.'

'I liked it,' he went on, 'Platoon too,' and continued: 'You know Khadaffi's troops were defeated in a battle in Chad the other day. Left a million dollars worth of military hardware sittin' right there in the desert. Did you know that?'

'No,' I said, 'I didn't know that.'

'That's some equipment.'

'It certainly is.'

'Course he's got a bunch of them chemical weapons all stashed away...nukes too.'

'Gaddaffi has nukes?' I asked incredulously.

'Shit yeah,' our friend replied, 'all kinds of warheads. We must take that sonofabitch out sooner rather than later.'

Americans like to fight. Any enemy will do.

We drove on in silence for awhile. The road wound away up through high passes and down again into steep valleys where the evening sun cast long shadows. Clumps of un-melted snow lined the roadside. It was cold. No traffic passed. The car engine made the only sound. I opened the window and a cold coyote called from somewhere deep in the woods. A lone deer crossed our path.

'Up hereabouts the Donner party got stranded,' said the man in the back, 'in the days before the gold rush, or maybe afterwards, a party of settlers heading for California from back east, Ohio I think it was or maybe Missouri. A whole lot of families, men, women and children in covered wagons. They beat off Indians, survived floods and rattlesnakes, 'til they got to these mountains.'

'And then what?'

'Then winter set in, coldest winter for almost fifty years. It snowed and snowed and they got completely lost and covered in, crossing the highest ridges. No real roads in them days, no radios nor snowploughs neither. They couldn't find a way through and the food ran out. First they killed the horses, and ate 'em. Then the dogs and whatever else they could find. A bunch of 'em started dying; old folks first, then the children, poor little mites, all shrivelled up, thin as skeletons in the snow.'

We were mesmerised in spite of ourselves. He continued: 'Some say they started eatin' the flesh off the dead bodies. Others say they began killing the weakest, before eatin' 'em.'

'That's disgusting,' said Jane with a shiver.

'A true story though, survival of the fittest,' said the trucker with relish, 'you do what you gotta do.'

'It was a great tragedy,' I said.

'A great American tragedy,' he emphasised, 'just a few managed to make it all the way down the mountain to Sacramento. Nobody would tell the real story, because of the terrible shame I guess. But gradually the rumours started flying, inquiries were made and people started pointing fingers. But the survivors carried the real, awful truth to their graves. Always known ever since as the Donner Party incident.'

Jane stole an uneasy look at me. I gave a half smile and then looked straight ahead. The sky was now an eggshell pink, with a star or two piercing the fading blue. The sun was setting and part of the sky was bright orange. Silence again settled over us like an invisible shroud.

'Say, ah, you mind pulling in for a second,' he said politely. 'I gotta go to the bathroom.' I stole another look at Jane, then looked back to the road. I could see some lights beginning to twinkle deep in the valley.

'There's a town down there,' I said, pointing.

'Can you hold out?' asked Jane. I thought I detected a tremor in her voice.

He said nothing for what seemed a long time. He shifted in his seat and I glanced in my mirror. He did not look happy.

'We'll be there in a ten minutes,' I said.

'Whatever,' he said gruffly.

Something, whatever it was, caused me to reconsider. Against my better judgement I stopped the car. The fellow clambered out with much grunting and stumbling. I snatched a look at Jane. She looked distressed. I left the engine running and put the full headlights on as the trucker shambled off into the barren woods. He'd taken his gas can with him, which I found odd, but did not say so. We waited, not wanting to speak to one another. A stray fox slunk across the headlights into the trees. I turned off the engine. There were hissing sounds of gases subsiding; liquids coagulating, trickling to standstill. I drummed my fingers on the dashboard. Jane looked at her watch. Suddenly the loud screech of a bald eagle destroyed the quiet and the startled bird floated grumpily away. We jumped like frightened rabbits in our seats and Jane clutched my arm. I turned the key. The engine roared into life. The trucker appeared in front of the windshield like a grinning ghoul. Jane gasped. He moved now with the speed of a dancer and was installed in the back seat before I could release the handbrake.

'You weren't thinkin' of leavin' me up here were you?' he inquired.

'I thought you'd gone off hunting or something,' I said.

'What took you so long?' asked Jane.

'I was lookin' for dead bodies,' he said nonchalantly.

I gunned the car forward, skimming around hairpin bends, as yawning chasms opened up on either side of the road. We plunged downwards with quickening heartbeats and bated breath. Nobody spoke until we reached the edge of the darkening town. I pulled up in front of a small motel with unseemly haste. I said this was as far as we were going. Jane threw me a look of relief and then looked back at our passenger. 'You'll have no trouble hitching another ride from here,' she said.

'You reckon,' he said sardonically and paused. Then he slowly got out, silhouetted against the ghostly white tips of the snow-topped Sierras. He squinted back at us like Clint Eastwood squinting at a varmint. Then he put his hand into the hole in the converted oil-can and slowlier still he drew out a pistol big enough to blow a hole through an elephant. He paused and looked to us for a reaction. We looked back, rigid, for what seemed like the last seconds of eternity. Then he waved the pistol around a little like you'd wave a baton. He patted it and leant in close: 'You should have one a' these little suckers,' he said confidentially, 'ain't nobody gonna mess with you when you're toting one of these.'

Then he straightened up and gave a little salute and said, 'God bless America.'

'God bless America,' we retorted eagerly.

Then he said: 'I sure hope Reagan gets Star Wars approved.'

We watched him walk away until he was out of sight. Then we got out silently and stretched our legs. I went into the men's room of an old western saloon where the walls were covered with advertisements from the end of the nineteenth century. One was for some kind of early toothpaste: "*Dr. Longs Tooth Powder - Thoroughly Cleans Teeth and Purifies Breath - Used By People of Refinement For 75 Years.*"

It was only then that I noticed that the shirt was clung to my back in a cold and clammy sweat.

When we got back in the car the night was dark and cold, but the sky was full of stars. We headed for San Franscisco on the interstate, which we caught on the edge of town. We said nothing for a long time. Hope and confidence seemed to leave our hearts like water from a tub. A feeling of all not being well that made us welter to what solar winds would blow. A shuddering of the ground beneath our feet.

ONE SUNDANCE KID

Pale stars shone down upon him. Venus first in the west. Then red Mars rising behind him. Sirius on the southern horizon, below the constellation of Orion. The roads now darkening. Soon more stars, no moon and August twilight disappearing. Autumn beckoning. He had come west from Gloucester, over Severn Bridge on ragged motorways through Wales. Past Newport, Swansea and on to the rocky coves of Fishguard and many black magical bedlams by the sea. All day from Brize Norton, past Cheltenham and the plains of Lambourn. Cheviot Hills. Tired now he was and still a long, long way to go. Ever westward. Onto the car ferry and pushing out into afternoon waves, rising and falling to Cork of his childhood, following the sun down the burning sky. Tired now but no sleeping. Drunks with crumpled beer cans snoring on the decks below. Cranky children, mangling greasy chips, making sleep impossible. Families doing their duty. The exigencies of the mundane. Late summer, yes, but not for him. No more. Goodbye to all that. Thirty years gone by since he left Haulbowline and Roches Point on the Inisfallen with his friends, all in the careless squanderings of their youth. Bobby Lowry gone off to England with a jaunty cigarette between his teeth. Gone off to conquer the world.

He had left her to clear his head. Her and the three teenagers. And wasn't sure if he'd go back. Endless rowing took its toll. The latest set-to was over money again. Some foolish venture gone wrong: an investment in a bar in Lambourn out near Richard Hannon's racing stables. He'd worked so hard at building the business but even harder on the gambling. He knew all the trainers: Hannon, Noel Chance, Nicky Henderson. They came in and out of his place all the time. He knew the bookies too and when times were good he was everyone's best friend. But sooner or later you always lost out to the bookies. There was only one J.P. McManus, one Sundance Kid, and it wasn't him, though once he might have been.

A loser, that's what she called him. A foolish dreamer, all over the shop. But what could he do? Time was running faster every year. Fifty-nine next birthday and each day harder to face. More aches, more fears. He still kept his lean, taut figure but closer inspection revealed irreversible lines around his eyes, and the inevitable greying of his once abundant, curling black locks. Once he had energy to burn but now he was tired all the time, worried all the time, though on the surface he seemed successful. He drove a Mercedes and their house was a big, five-bed, faux-mansion in an upmarket suburb. When he went back to Ireland, which was rarely now, he was thought of as a big-shot which was hardly true. He kept up appearances like other emigrants, though the reality wouldn't stand up to a forensic examination. But he liked to escape to Ireland. He was escaping now.

Docking at Ringaskiddy, the brand new ferry had disgorged its load of weary travellers. All around, the sunset made the islands and inlets of the huge harbour golden in the magic hour. Late, feathered waders and divers hunted in the evening stillness: lone herons, storm petrels hurtling low over the glassy waters of the estuary. Sooty shearwaters, gannets, egrets and spoonbills, gathering sustenance for their autumn migrations. Cobh cathedral caught in a last noose of sunlight. Jack Doyle, the Gorgeous Gael had started here, from here the Titanic sailed. Before her the Jeanie Johnston: coffin ship crossing the Atlantic with poor, lost famine souls. Cork city always surprised him with its watery face. Venice of the west. He drove on into the gathering twilight, over new roads that were boreens when he set out for England in 1967. Familiar landmarks surrounded with new housing estates and cranes on the skyline. Bishopstown, the Viaduct, onwards to Crossbarry where his father fought for Ireland eighty years before. But that was worlds away from this swaggering new Ireland. And who was Tom Lowry now they'd never know? And he, Bobby his son? A fading star.

He stopped in the village where he went to school way out west, where he hoped things still hadn't changed too much. Where on the off-chance someone might still know him and time might have been turning somewhat slower. He pulled into the back yard of a public house. When he walked in there was a man with a balding pate and a thickening waistline sitting at the counter. He wore a dark suit without a tie and he nursed a lonely pint of stout. He looked at Bobby and then looked away. There was a picture of a Cork hurler on the wall, in full flight, all grace and action. It was a dark, dreary place with a little snug running off it. Garish banners advertising beer hung like a clothesline across the muddy-brown ceiling. There was a pop song playing on an invisible radio over a vibrating speaker. It was about eight o'clock on this late August evening and the place was empty as a grave. The gloomy interior filled him with foreboding. The charm of the old country pub that he remembered from his childhood had died many years ago and the skeletal remains grinned back at him, mocking his memories. The owner came in. Bobby vaguely recognised him from somewhere in the past. He wasn't sure if he was recognised in turn. The owner had grey hair but he was still tall and straight and retained his good looks somehow.

'How are you?' he asked Bobby without enthusiasm

'Not bad.'

'What can I get you?'

'Give me a Guinness.'

'A pint?'

'Yes.'

Bobby pulled over a tall stool and sat on it. He looked idly around. There was a wintry chill to the place and no fire lighting. Just a cheap, electric radiator turned off. The glasses didn't look too clean either. The owner washed a few and then fiddled with the radio dial. A young deejay with a Cork accent pretending to be American announced the name of the singer as the song finished.

'What station is that?' asked Bobby.

'County Sound,' said the owner.

'A Dublin station is it?'

'Not at all,' said the owner, 'tis a Cork station. We have all our own stuff around here now, satellite television, internet broadband, the lot.'

There was a soccer match playing on the large, wide-screened television high on the wall. The sound was turned down but he recognised Manchester United.

'Things have come a long way,' said Bobby.

'Yerra what,' said the owner, denoting a universe of achievements.

Silence again. The deejay was talking about some impending events: Westlife coming to town, REM the following week. It was all happening.

He was aware of a pair of eyes watching him intently. He stole a half-glance toward the other customer sitting skeways across from him on the other arm of the counter. Bobby smiled and said: 'Good weather.'

The man continued to stare at him and said nothing. The ghost of a smile twisted his lips, positive or negative Bobby couldn't tell. Then the man said suddenly: 'You haven't changed a bit.'

'Huh,' said Bobby aware of the irony.

'Still the same oul smoocher,' said the other and he began to cackle with hoarse, sour laughter that ended in a spluttering, hacking cough. Bobby was nonplussed, desperately trying to remember the once handsome face, now raddled, pockmarked, puffed, like a map of broken dreams.

'How are things in England?' continued the toper, levering his elbows on the counter. 'Not bad,' said Bobby evenly, 'but things are very good hereabouts I believe.'

'By all accounts,' said the man with sarcasm.

'Never better,' said the barman, eager not to let the side down.

The drinker lit a cigarette and blew the smoke in his direction. 'You don't remember me,' he said, and looked offended.

'You're face is familiar,' said Bobby diplomatically, 'but I couldn't put a name on you to save my life.'

'Familiar my arse,' said the man, 'wasn't I one class behind you in school, with Master Kelly, the hard bastard.'

Bobby stared into the crystal ball of the past. School and Master Kelly were a thousand light years ago, across oceans, and crowded cities and a hundred false dawns and disappointments. The crystal long since grown opaque. He shook his head and gave up.

'Joe Delaney,' said the barman, bailing him out.

'Jesus,' said Bobby, 'Joe Delaney,' and rose and went to shake his hand, 'I wouldn't know you from a ton of bricks.'

'Christ, but you're some bollox,' said Joe, half-mocking, half-angry and leant back to regard Bobby's neat, navy jacket, pressed trousers and shiny shoes.

Bobby again tried to bridge the gulf of years and disentangle the twisted whorls of fate that had sent them spinning out like stars in an expanding universe away from the little village, the slow meandering river, the green hills and the wide fields of home; but like ships with tattered sails they had passed too far beyond each other's hail. They both were now pretending.

'Fill a pint for that man,' said Joe.

The barman drew down another glass and Bobby and Joe stood captive in the gloom and wondered what to say next. When the storm of the porter had subsided in the glass Joe said: 'The

Silverlake Ballroom, d'you remember the night you got stuck in a fight over the Sweeney girl with the fellas from Bantry?'

'I do,' said Bobby trying to conjure the face of the teenage hairdresser who'd raised the blood of many young men of twenty and set them at each other's throats like stags in spring.

'You were the lucky man I was behind you that night,' said Joe 'or you'd have been carried out on a stretcher, or maybe a coffin.'

'Quite right,' said Bobby in a haze.

'The Silverlake was some spot,' said the barman, with gravitas.

'Yerra for Christ's sake,' said Joe, 'didn't you have the best bands in the country playing in the Silverlake: Joe Mac and the Dixies, The Clipper Carlton...'

'The Freshmen...'

'The Royal,' added Joe, 'Brendan Bowyer and the Royal..."*Do the hucklebuck do the hucklebuck, if you don't know how to do it then your outa luck...*" ' He sang in a hoarse, cracked voice, as tuneless as a braying donkey and then said: 'But you're the man for the singing Bobby, give us a blast of *Wooden Heart.*'

Bobby smiled ruefully and said, 'I haven't sung that song for twenty years.'

'Christ, but you're some bollox,' said Joe again, 'what a waste of talent.' And he said to the barman: 'You should have seen this fella when he was twenty-one. Jack Doyle wasn't in it, wouldn't hold a candle to him.' And he sang: "*Can't you see I love you please don't break my heart in two...*" Give us the sad verse will you?'

Bobby felt like he was being pulled backwards into a place where the sun shone bright all around him, when he was twenty-one and the son of the morning star. The golden boy of the surrounding territory and all the girls in thrall; asked to sing at every concert and cockfight and dance at every crossroads and ballroom of romance. The life and soul of every party; liked and praised by older men, adored by teenage boys and girls. On magic Sundays dancing the night away, basking in the glow of admiring glances. Lines of love-lorn girls with powder and lipstick, drinking bottles of orange juice, locked in lines of rigid segregation, ogling him across the dancefloor. Oh, how sweet it was to pretend to be a big-shot for an hour or two. Stealing furtive, hard-won kisses. Inveigling some forward-thinking girl outside to loiter under a wanton moon. The music of the band floating across the carpark, hard-chaws smoking in the shadows. Boastful claims of conquest that proved insubstantial in the bright light of day. Giving the impression that he had prospects, was going places. But always found out in the end, seen through, intentions queried, amorous advances cut off midstream. Wending his weary way homeward and dreaming of a better life, with swimming pools and girls in bikinis, like Elvis in *G.I. Blues.*

'Bobby Lowry,' Joe was saying to the barman, 'Bobby Lowry should have been in pictures. But you know what that fella's problem was? I'll tell you what it was: too bloody lazy by half. I'm telling you straight.'

And he gave Bobby a dig in the ribs and drank again. And both drank again and there followed a silence that might have been too painful to break. For the road back home was hard to follow but the road downhill was an easy road.

'Where are you nowadays?' asked the barman politely, 'London is it?'

'I'm in a small town in the middle of England.'

'And were you in America?'

'I was there too.'

'Really, and what did you do there?'

'Oh, this and that,' said Bobby. 'I tried some singing. Then I went to Hollywood for a couple of years. I got some small parts in pictures.'

Bobby said this so casually that the barman, though all agog, thought he must be joking. 'I'm not joking,' laughed Bobby, 'I only wish I could say I was more successful.'

'Hollywood?' repeated the barman unable to comprehend the concept, ''tis hard to believe a fella from around here went to Hollywood, not to mind being in pictures.'

'There you are,' said Bobby and smiled a world-weary smile.

'This fella has what you might call a chequered history,' said Joe cryptically.

'No more than yourself,' laughed Bobby.

'Yerra God help us sure I never left this little village, except to go to Cork for the county final.'

'For a man who never went anywhere you know a lot about everything, me included.'

'An undiscovered Homer, that's what they'd call me around here, if they knew who Homer was,' and Joe was off laughing at his own doomed wit again.

'You never lost it,' said Bobby.

'Never found it you mean,' said Joe with a sad look and shook his resigned head. He looked at Bobby again and looked away: 'Some of us never made it, never played for Cork.'

'Never made the money,' said the barman.

'Never married the beauty queen,' shrugged Joe.

'Christ, we're not finished yet,' said Bobby, 'where's your spirit man?'

'Indeed we are,' said Joe sadly, 'you'd want to have it all done by twenty-five, all behind you by twenty five.'

There was a pause as a dripping tap made the only sound in the gloom. The silent TV screen flickered its jaded images of soccer players and clichés.

'Time moves fast,' the barman said.

'Like a shot,' said Joe, 'and for some of us it might as well have been standing still; but you made the best of it Bobby, you've seen a fair share of the world.'

'I have,' said Bobby.

'And which part did you like the best?' asked the barman.

Bobby thought for a moment and then leant in on the bar and said: 'You mightn't believe this, but of all the places I've been I like this place best of all.' Joe looked incredulously at him and gave a snort: 'Like hell you do?'

'I never thought I'd think it or say it for that matter, but it's the truth.'

Joe stood up and weaved uncertainly towards the toilet and said he was going to water the pony. He came back smiling, a mystical smile. Peaceful. As if he were already looking into the next life: 'The faster we go the slower we get,' he said.

'You reckon?' said Bobby.

'There's yourself now with all your *gaisces* and achievements, not to mention your money, and then there's me without a shilling, but we're all back here at the end of the day. Back where we started from.' And Joe thought this all very funny and laughed his wheezing, ironic, bittersweet laugh that fell on ghost's ears in the shadows.

'What have you been at yourself?' Bobby eventually asked Joe.

'Devil a much then,' said Joe.

'Am I right in thinking you were in line for the hardware business. Didn't your father keep a shop?'

'He did,' said Joe, 'but my heart wasn't in it. I let the younger brother have it.'

His nose twitched and he searched for further mischief, sizing Bobby up: 'And besides, a push from the grave never did anyone any good. No, my heart was never in it. So I stayed here close to home, mornings, evenings, nights. I'd hear the river and watch the grass grow. I'd hear dogs barking, I'd see bats, night owls. I'd read a bit of Homer maybe. Often when I couldn't sleep I'd wander up to the foot of Mount Gabriel and I swear I could hear the old heroes crossing the fields, with bandoliers and rifles at the trail: the boys who beat the Black and Tans, they were the men, eh? Not a couple of *súmaires* like us?'

He paused and then said sadly: 'And sometimes I'd see the school children coming through the barley with the afternoon sun on their faces in July and I wished I was young again.'

Bobby stared at Joe and was sad for a stymied heart and a man who could paint with words.

'I was never like you,' Joe said. 'I was always afraid. I'd have to steel myself against the long nights and the boredom with nothing happening. No excitement, only the humdrum, the mundane. The quotidien if you like. And the strain, especially the strain.'

'The strain of what?' asked Bobby.

'You were dealt a good hand by the Lord, Bobby,' said Joe, 'things came easy to you. You could drive on, up the middle. 'Twas no bother to you. As for me, sure I settled for listening to the Light Programme on the BBC with the wet battery, and my mother telling me to change my clothes on Sunday.' Bobby nodded and was lost in reverie and the barman went over and lit the electric fire. Its single bar glowed like a distant quasar.

Bobby had no mother to tell him change his clothes. She died when he was ten and he scarcely knew her. And in quieter moments he sensed her loss. Maybe felt rudderless with only the harsh but well-intentioned hand of Tom to guide him. Rough and ready. Sowing potatoes and ploughing fields with heavy horses. Hoeing sugarbeet in springtime and his fingers freezing as he pulled the swollen beets in bleak, sleet-blown November. Time hurrying faster every year and he getting no younger. And no richer. In his late twenties and the roles of father and son long since reversed. Now it was he who called the shots and gave the orders: 'Shut up you old fool and stop slobbering your tea.'

And poor Tom with no choice but to be quiet and do as he was bid. Pushing seventy, becoming weak and stumbling. Becoming an old man. And Bobby all he had. And the young man's restless heart, fighting his chains, his head filled with fantasies of what the world might hold, what the future could bring. If only he took wing.

As Joe said again: 'No, I always said a push from the grave never helped anyone,' Bobby returned to the present.

'What do you mean a push from the grave?' he asked.

'Well, like you got,' said Joe.

'Me, what did I get?'

'Sure the world knows what you got, from the oul fella: the farm, on a plate.'

Bobby felt uneasy. Wondering how to reply. He kept his silence. Then he drained the last of his glass and looked at his watch. He slapped Joe on the shoulder with an old familiar touch and said he'd better be going. Joe slowly shook his hand and then Bobby saluted the barman before walking through the door.

'That shook him,' said the barman

'I didn't say anything that hasn't already been said,' said Joe.

Twilight was nearly gone and night was falling as Bobby left the village and drove on slowly. As the road rose, like a rising crane shot in a film scene, a spectacular panorama of sea, islands, castles and boats appeared in breathtaking clarity. How well he knew this view, but each time he returned it became more deeply etched on his psyche. There were the Skeams, Hare Island, Carthy's Islands, Sherkin and the round, camel-hump of Cape Clear on the horizon. And down the long bay, subdivided by serried lines of fish-farming nets, his eye was carried to the proud, high Fastnet Rock that flashed a welcome to weary sailors all night long. On the foreshore, two solitary swans glided towards a pier and two dark seabirds' cries broke the stillness with a warm, remembered pain.

There were several new houses on the road: big, stone-faced mansions, probably owned by Germans. There were new bungalows too, built by the locals. You could usually tell. The foreigners could afford to splash out and spend a lot on finishing. The locals found it hard to compete despite the boom-times taking hold. When he came to his own place he got quite a shock. The farmyard was gone, the old famine cottage gone, and the house where he was born transformed from an old plastered, three-bedroomed dwelling into something strange and new and modern; with seven bedrooms, festooned with balustrades and conservatories and arches. The surrounding field where his pony used to graze now a lawn; the little hedges from the iron gate on the road cut down and replaced by a profusion of flower-beds with Japanese names. The effect was not displeasing but it was home no more. Hard as he looked he could uncover no trace of his childhood, all vanished like a slate wiped clean. There was a Mercedes 500 parked inside large, electronic gates on the gravelled yard. He debated with himself whether to go in and introduce himself, but if the inside was like the outside, then all vestiges of Bobby Lowry, his father Tom and his mother Mary, and the hard-scrabble life they led, would surely have been also erased, consigned to oblivion with not even a photograph to record that they had been there at all. Such a possibility he chose not to face. He still had his memories and while he had them he was alive, though running on empty for a few years now.

He drove on slowly up the hill past the house and attempted to shrug off tears of regret, tears of time. When he came to the last field where the bounds ditch ran he got out and looked back down at the buildings nestling in the valley under the hill. He could hear like only yesterday his father's voice as he came across the farmyard that rainy, long gone day as Bobby was finishing the milking; and his father saying: 'I'm going to make the place over to you.'

And Bobby stopping, surprised, and asking: 'What?'

And Tom saying: 'I went to Collins, the solicitor, I signed it over to you lock, stock and barrel.'

'You did?'

'I did. For better or for worse, I did.'

And Bobby remembered staring into the future as a pride of hungry cats nearly upscuttled a bucket of milk, and he kicking them away. A whirlwind of thoughts going through his head. His place now? Could he do as he liked or was this a bribe, or worse maybe a trap? What about his hatching plans for leaving, and the bright lights and the big city?

But only saying, 'That's fine so,' and then straining the bucket of warm, creamy milk into the shining, silver churn, watching the froth collecting in bubbles as the milk gurgled. Sang as it hit the bottom. Smelling the sweet-grass smell of the milk and when the bucket was empty, licking a glob of cream from his fingers.

Random memories hit him thick and fast: after Tom's unexpected gesture a noticeable springing in his step. His voice echoing in song across the townlands, like the voice of Orpheus singing to light up the gloom of the approaching winter. And winter coming in like a lion. Howling gales in November, trees falling and the roads becoming rivers swept away. Then December and hard frosts and the lonesome call of the pilibeen and the snipe; and the yellow bittern foraging on frozen lakes. Then the snows of January, cattle hungry in the uplands, Bobby struggling through snowdrifts with haynets to feed the bellowing beasts. His fingers frostbitten, icicles forming on his nose. His elation on becoming a landlord quickly dissipating in the cold winds of reality blowing against his backside month after month. Surely there was a better life? Maybe he would go to England for awhile. He had heard there was good money on the buildings of Birmingham and London. And he could afford to go now. He had an asset to realize. Even if things did not work out he could use the money and maybe have a crack at singing for his supper?

The unthinkable already foremost in his mind before he was consciously aware of it. And quietly rationalising the betrayal of his father. The deal done with a man from the next parish before telling Tom. Choosing a man who was fond of money and land. Who valued land over loyalty. Some others might have baulked at the suggestion, indeed some were scandalised. Some old comrades of Tom Lowry who remembered the struggles he came through refused to speak to Bobby ever again. And Bobby gone with the money almost before anyone was aware that he had sold the farm. Eaten bread was soon forgotten, and in the bright bars of Birmingham and giddy among the racegoers at Cheltenham or Royal Ascot, the pain and loneliness of an old man with a walking stick, taking shelter from an angry squall under a blackthorn bush, on a lonely road by the sea, was not something to be dwelt on overlong. Summer was on the way and Bobby would be back to visit. But not just yet.

He got back in the car and drove down to the foreshore. The past and present now all coalescing. Old Tom dying and he standing at the grave talking to the dead. And furtive recriminating eyes. Leaving his father to be cared for by strangers and his father lonesome for his son's return, dying of a broken heart: the man who fought for his country. Tears of guilt every time he stood in conversation with the dead. Everyone he knew as a boy, now dead. The dead more real than the living.

Where had the years gone and whither all the money? A cache of money emptying from his pockets, like leaves blowing off a beech tree in the first autumn storm. The singing and the dancing and romancing: London and New York and out to California and back again. Time hurrying, years passing. Babies' cries and the burdens of house and home. The future receding ever faster and every time his reach exceeding his grasp.

Out along the bay the high cliffs of Cape Clear hulked somewhere in the darkness. An enormous darkness swept every now and then by the lonely pencil of the Fastnet light. He walked, cloaked from accusing eyes and then his fingers felt the solid, reassuring pier. He heard small boats bobbing and clunking against each other on the rising tide. And the smell of deadly nightshade brought him peace by these untrammelled waters, until he no longer heard the sorrowing cries of those dark birds of shame.